"I want you, Tayl...

The colored lights p... oasis glittering in his eyes. "Hearing you say you want me, too, doesn't generate a single patronizing thought."

Staring into his eyes, seeing so much emotion reflected, Taylor swallowed. "What does it do?"

"Makes me want to kiss you even more than I already did."

Jack wanted to kiss her.

She'd known that.

Still, his words thrilled her, made her want to jump up and down and dance around the sandpit like a giddy schoolgirl. His words also made her want to take off running again. As far as her feet would take her, because Lord help her at the things his admission did to her insides.

"We just met yesterday," she reminded, herself as much as him.

His gaze held hers. "I haven't forgotten."

Her heart slammed against her rib cage so hard that surely he felt the impact of each beat. "It's too soon."

His thumb stroked across her jawline. "I know."

But even as the words left his mouth, she leaned over and brushed her lips against his.

Dear Reader,

Over a decade ago a music festival began taking over my small hometown for a week each summer. For years I've mulled over writing a story set at just such a music festival, but I had to wait for the perfect characters. When Dr. Jack Morgan appeared in my vivid imagination, he insisted that a music festival background be his story and for me to find him a just-right heroine.

Nurse Taylor Hall has spent the last year putting her life back together. When she signs on to work a music festival's medical tent, the last thing she's thinking about is meeting a man. But the melody of romance entices and so does Jack. But can Taylor risk falling for a free-spirited man who dances to the beat of his own song when she knows he's destined to leave?

I hope you enjoy Jack and Taylor's story as much as I did writing it. I'd had years of experience—I mean research!—to create my setting and it was so much fun putting it on paper.

Happy reading and rock on.

Janice

A NURSE TO TAME
THE ER DOC

———

JANICE LYNN

HARLEQUIN® MEDICAL ROMANCE™

Recycling programs
for this product may
not exist in your area.

ISBN-13: 978-1-335-64168-7

A Nurse to Tame the ER Doc

First North American Publication 2019

Copyright © 2019 by Janice Lynn

HARLEQUIN®
www.Harlequin.com

Printed in U.S.A.

Books by Janice Lynn

Harlequin Medical Romance

Christmas in Manhattan

A Firefighter in Her Stocking

Flirting with the Doc of Her Dreams
New York Doc to Blushing Bride
Winter Wedding in Vegas
Sizzling Nights with Dr. Off-Limits
It Started at Christmas…
The Nurse's Baby Secret
The Doctor's Secret Son
A Surgeon to Heal Her Heart
Heart Surgeon to Single Dad
Friend, Fling, Forever?

Visit the Author Profile page
at Harlequin.com for more titles.

**Janice won the National Readers' Choice Award
for her first book,
*The Doctor's Pregnancy Bombshell***

To Dr. Jay Trussler for his insight on working medical for a major music festival.
Thanks for the tour, the stories and for answering all my questions.

CHAPTER ONE

YES! NURSE TAYLOR HALL mentally pumped her fist in the air as she looked across the Rockin' Tyme music festival medical tent at the tall man wearing a "Medical Staff" T-shirt and navy shorts.

Yes. Yes. *Yes.*

Her body had noticed a man.

Sure, the current tingles were just sparks of physical attraction, but as she'd thought good old-fashioned lust a thing of the past at the age of twenty-five, Taylor cherished the incoming zings.

She wasn't dead inside after all.

Her ex hadn't accomplished quite as much as she'd given him credit for this past year. Thank God.

Seeming to sense someone was watching him, the medical staff hottie glanced up from the clipboard he'd been studying and met Taylor's gaze with eyes so brilliant she questioned if they were colored contacts. She was positive she'd never met him, but recognition flashed in his baby blues and a huge smile lit his face.

Wow. Just wow.

Awareness sparks burst into blistering red-hot flames.

Crazy that something as simple as physical attraction could make her feel so ecstatic, especially since she wasn't interested in a relationship, but Taylor credited the heat as a sign she was healing. She truly had progressed from the beaten down woman she'd been at her divorce a year ago.

Of course she had. She was a strong, independent woman who didn't need a man to hold her hand. She held her future. No one else.

The job interview she'd gone to earlier that day had been yet another sign of how far she'd come. She'd moved on from the past and was taking charge of her life in new and exciting ways.

Curious at the man who'd awakened her libido when she'd been so oblivious to the opposite sex for so long, she took in his features. He wasn't the most handsome man she'd ever seen, not even close to her ex's Hollywood perfect good looks. But there was something about this guy that had drawn her attention the moment she'd stepped into the Rockin' Tyme music festival medical tent, which was abuzz with activity.

His shoulder-length, sun-kissed brown hair, pulled back with a rubber band, and skin told a story of someone who loved to be outdoors and spent a lot of time doing so. Someone who didn't worry about his outward appearance, but who'd been blessed with natural good looks. Friendly face and eyes, great smile, nice body, and if he was who she thought he was, he was Amy's friend.

Her bestie had never liked Taylor's ex.

Amy had said she would know Dr. Jackson Morgan when she saw him. Everything inside her had "known" this man—or sure wanted to.

Taylor smiled at the hunk standing twenty or so feet away. Would he think her certifiable if she walked over to thank him?

He immediately put his clipboard down on the table in front of him and crossed the tent. Had he read her mind and was going to say, "You're welcome."?

Ha. She'd hug him for real.

She fought back another smile and told herself to get a grip. Just because her body suddenly remembered it was female, it didn't mean she would dare act on those zings. After the raking over the coals Neil had put her through, she had planned to avoid men forever. Not all men were like Neil. She knew that. But no matter how many sparks and tingles, no matter how excited she was that her insides weren't dead, when it came to men, her brain warned her to steer clear.

Men weren't worth the trouble.

Once upon a time she'd thought she needed one. The last year had taught her she was just fine without one.

Better than fine.

"Taylor, right?" He grinned, causing happy lines to fan out from his eyes.

Great smile, she thought again as she nodded. Genuine, not calculated. A smile that radiated as much from his eyes as his mouth.

"I'm not a crazy stalker." He chuckled. "Amy Sellars told me to be on the lookout for you."

Another wave of disappointment that Amy wasn't there hit Taylor. Not that Amy could help it that her grandmother had fallen and broken a hip two states away, but Taylor had really been looking forward to catching up with her best friend. Amy had come to Louisville last summer immediately following the finalization of Taylor's divorce, but that seemed forever ago, and Taylor hadn't done much more than cry.

Tears for lost dreams and tears of happiness that she'd escaped Neil's controlling, abusive hands.

"Amy has a picture of the two of you on her fireplace mantel," the medical staffer continued. "I recognized you immediately."

Taylor knew the photo he spoke of. She had the same one displayed at the tiny apartment she'd leased following moving out of Neil's sprawling showplace. The photo was a close-up following her and Amy's nurse pinning ceremony. Their smiles had been huge, as had their dreams for the future.

Her university roommate had tried for years to get Taylor to work the infamous annual festival that took place in her hometown. Taylor finally had and now Amy wasn't even in town.

Agreeing to work the music festival had been more about spending time with her friend than the generous sum she'd be paid for her three twelve-hour shifts. But the extra pay wasn't a bad thing.

Still, if her job interview that morning had gone as well as she thought, they'd soon have lots of catch-up time.

If all went according to plan, she'd be living with her former roomie yet again. Amy had tried to get Taylor to relocate last summer, but Taylor had needed to put her life back together on her own. She'd needed to stand on her own two feet. It would have been too easy to let Amy take over and just have gone through the motions.

Which was what Taylor had done her whole life.

Gone with the flow. Done what had been expected. First with her parents and then with Neil. She'd never stepped outside the boundaries they'd set. Not until she'd left Neil and filed for divorce.

She was a work in progress but was happy with the woman emerging from the wreck she'd been. She was still peeling back the layers of years of toeing the line, but most mornings she liked the person staring back at her in the mirror.

"Amy was excited you're working the festival."

Taylor's attention zoned back in on the man who was studying her. The man who'd been inside her friend's apartment.

Was Amy dating him? She hadn't said so, but her friend had been enthusiastic when talking about him. She'd gotten the impression Amy had been hinting at a possible romance between Taylor and the doctor during the music festival, hints Taylor had ignored because she'd not been interested in a man since long before her divorce. She had no plans for a relationship and, even if she had, she'd just as soon have her fingernails ripped out as to get involved with another doctor.

He held out his hand. "Jackson Morgan."

He'd introduced himself without using his medical title, something her ex would never have done. Kudos for that.

"Nice to meet you, Jackson." Taylor returned

his smile, shook his hand, and marveled at the tingles of awareness that shot up her arm at the warmth of his hand.

Men sworn off or not, the guy was electric.

"My friends call me Jack," he commented as she pulled her hand free from his.

"Jack." Taylor let the name roll off her tongue. "You're the hotshot traveling emergency medicine doctor Amy works with at Rockin' Tyme each year."

"My reputation has preceded me yet again." His eyes danced with mischief.

Taylor tried to recall what her friend had said but couldn't pull up much. She'd thought Amy matchmaking when she'd gone on and on about the doctor they'd be working with at the festival. Taylor had been excited about seeing her best friend, not about meeting a man. What had Amy said?

"Good looking, funny—can't wait for you to meet him. Think you'll really like him. He's the best."

"Nothing bad," she admitted, smiling at Jack. If he and Amy were an item, then good for her friend and even better for this guy. Any man would be lucky to call Amy his own. If he was good to her friend then, doctor or not, Taylor would hug him for a totally different reason than the one that had hit her upon first seeing him.

"Good to know she's not talking smack about me." He glanced around the medical tent, his gaze skimming over the cots along a far side where a group of workers was chatting. "I'll miss her being here. Hated to hear about her grand-mother."

"That makes two of us. She convinced me to sign on and now she's not here." Following his gaze out the open flaps of the tent, she took a deep breath. "I can't help but wonder what she's gotten me into."

"No worries. She made me promise to take good care of you."

Taylor's gaze cut to his. "Oh?"

He grinned, and his eyes crinkled. Wow, such a great smile. "At least a dozen times—and that was just this morning."

Taylor smiled. Her friend always had looked out for her.

If only Taylor had listened better.

Jack working as a traveling doctor must cre-ate relationship problems. "Do you get to see her often?"

"I see Amy several times a week," he an-swered, looking a little surprised at her ques-tion. "I liked Warrenville so much I temporarily relocated here a couple of months ago to fill in for a doctor on an extended medical leave."

"Oh." Had her perky friend influenced that

decision? Good for Amy. Taylor was happy for her but why hadn't Amy told her? Maybe her friend had been afraid of jinxing whatever was happening. Still, that Amy hadn't mentioned their relationship made Taylor sad as once upon a time they'd shared everything.

Then again, hadn't she put on a face for her friend for years? Not wanting Amy to know the truth behind her miserable marriage?

"Have you met the rest of the crew?" Jack asked, drawing her focus back.

Taylor shook her head. "Do you already know each other?"

"Mostly," he admitted. "There are always a few new people, but most of us come back each year. It's a tradition. A lot of the staff are locals, but some do travel. It's a good bunch who work the medical tent. You'll enjoy hanging with us."

Either way, it was just for a few days so she'd survive. She'd survived worse. Besides, wasn't she all about new life experiences and stepping outside the box she'd lived in for so long?

"How did you get involved with the festival?" she asked, glancing out the front of the medical tent to the "oasis" that was located about a hundred yards away. Fake palm trees planted in a huge sand pit with splash pools for play and cooling down during the hot July heat.

This was definitely a new life experience.

"Music festivals are in my blood. My grandparents were hippies and actually met at Woodstock." Grinning, he made a peace sign with his fingers. "I've been going to festivals since before I could walk. My parents thought I'd grow up to be a musician—or a gypsy," he added, chuckling. "But medicine called me. Since I left med school, I've worked numerous festivals every year so it's a balance of work and play. Makes me feel I've evolved from those days of driving across the country with a car load of buddies with nothing on our brains except good music and good times."

"Sounds like fun." Taylor couldn't imagine the carefree trips he was describing. Her strict parents had barely gotten by and Taylor had had her first job at fifteen. She'd been working ever since. Even then, there'd never been money or time for cross-country road trips to soak up the sun and music. For a short while early in their relationship she'd felt happiness and a sense of peace with Neil. After their wedding, nothing had been carefree during those torturous two years.

"The best." Jack grinned, but something was off in his smile as he looked back out over the festival. "Let me give you the low down on how things will run the next few days in the tent and introduce you to the others."

Taylor was scheduled to work Thursday and Friday from four a.m. to four p.m. and on Sunday from four p.m. to four a.m. on Monday.

"We're on the same work schedule," she commented, spotting Jack's name on the schedule near hers.

"It's not a coincidence," he admitted, grinning. "Amy and you are purposely on the same schedule as mine. Didn't see a reason to change it when Amy cancelled at the last minute. How else can I keep my promise if you and I are on different schedules?"

"How indeed?" At least she was guaranteed a friendly face during her shifts because Jack seemed to always smile. He was the most laid-back person she'd encountered in a long time. Maybe ever. "Do most of the crew sleep or participate in the festival activities during their down time?"

"A mixture. Most take in a few concerts. But some hang around the camping area or leave the farm to check out local attractions."

"Is that how you fell in love with the area?"

He hesitated a minute, then said, "Amy had a lot to do with that."

If she'd had any doubt, there was her confirmation that there was something between her friend and Jack. She fought back a fresh twinge of disappointment that he was taken, reminded herself he was a doctor and she wasn't interested anyway. Plus, she truly was pleased for Amy. She'd just met Jack and she already liked him.

"I'm happy for you."

He stared at her a moment, then his eyes lit with surprise. "Not sure what Amy told you…" he chuckled as he continued "…but we're just friends. I'm sure she feels the same."

Heat flooded her face. Just friends. "Oh."

"You thought she and I were more?"

Oh, good grief. Her face burned. Her ears burned. Could the ground just please open and swallow her now?

"Well, you did mention you were at her apartment," she reminded him, trying to explain why she'd thought what she had.

"At a party she threw for a co-worker." His eyes danced with merriment. "Nothing nearly as exciting as what you were imagining."

"Too bad for you. Amy is a great catch." All true, but even as she said it she had to remind herself yet again that she was not interested in becoming involved, especially not with someone in the same profession as Neil. No way.

"I agree," Jack assured her. "Amy has been talking with my best friend for the past couple of weeks. Nothing would make me happier than if the two of them continue to hit it off."

Amy hadn't mentioned the best friend either.

Had Taylor and her bestie really grown that far apart over the past few years? She'd been so wrapped up in trying to make her marriage work and ashamed of the situation in which she'd found herself that she'd not invested time into their friendship. Yet Amy had always been there any time Taylor had called, like when she'd finally filed for divorce.

Guilt hit her. She'd do better. Lots better. It had taken her the past year to build a foundation of who she was, who she wanted to be.

"So, nothing between the two of you?" she double-checked, just to be sure she'd understood correctly.

"Friendship."

"I'm sorry." She really was. Amy was the best person she knew and deserved the best of everything. Maybe Jack's friend would prove to be worthy.

"I'm not."

"Why's that?" Her gaze locked with his and her breath caught. His eyes sparkled like sunshine dancing across lake water.

"Let's just say—" he was looking at her as if she were the sweetest soda pop he'd ever wanted to taste "—I've been looking forward to meeting you."

Awareness filled Taylor. Awareness that had nothing to with anything except good old-fashioned girl meets boy. Good grief. Her body didn't seem to care about his taboo medical credentials and her ban against men.

Eek. Maybe she shouldn't have been quite so ecstatic about her libido's revival.

When Taylor's brow lifted, her expression cautious, Jack chided himself for his admission. If he wasn't careful, she was going to think he really was a stalker.

Was it considered stalking if her best friend had talked about her so much Jack had been looking forward to meeting her for weeks?

Longer.

She'd caught his eye years ago the first time he'd seen her photo. Something in her eyes, her smile had called to him. He'd been sad to learn she was married. When Amy had mentioned her divorced best friend was coming to work Rockin' Tyme, he'd been intrigued, wondering if the real deal would intrigue him as much as her photo.

She did.

Taylor Hall was a beautiful woman. Thick almost platinum blonde hair, golden brown eyes, pouty lips, and a body he had to force himself not to think about. She was easily one of the most beautiful women he'd ever seen, but it was something in her eyes that had snagged his attention years ago and refused to let go even now that he'd met her in person.

He suspected that although her outside packaging was beautiful, the real beauty was hidden away like a secret treasure.

Jack introduced her to the crew, all of whom were friendly but really brightened when he told them she was Amy's friend.

"Shame Amy's not going to be here this year," one said, giving her hand a hearty shake.

"Sorry to hear about her grandmother," another commented.

Robert, a paramedic from a couple of counties away, grinned, stuck his hand out to Taylor, and eyed her in much the way Jack probably had.

"Tell me I'm the luckiest guy on the planet and you're single?"

Jack's gaze immediately shifted to Taylor's to see how she'd respond to the man's blatant flirting.

Eyes wide with surprise, she eyed him, then laughed softly. "I'm single."

Looking upwards, Robert made a thankful gesture.

"But not looking for a music festival hook-up, if that's what you mean by lucky."

"A pity," Robert said, eyeing her with a huge grin. "You and I could have had a lot of fun."

Jack liked the paramedic, but currently he

wanted to throttle the guy. "Ignore Robert. The sun gets to him real quick and he talks out of his head."

Taylor laughed. "That explains a lot."

"Besides, certain staff interactions aren't encouraged."

Robert eyed Jack as if he'd grown an extra head, and no wonder. "Never heard of it being discouraged, not here."

There had been romances pop up between staff. Jack himself had met a few interesting women over the years that he'd enjoyed getting to know. But he didn't want Robert having the wrong idea about Taylor.

She was off limits.

Next thing you knew, Jack was going to be beating his chest and acting like a fool. Shaking his head, he chuckled. "Okay, Casanova, back off and let me introduce her to Duffy."

He and Duffy had worked numerous events together and he genuinely liked the fifty-something travel nurse who craved adventure almost as much as Jack.

"Duffy Reynolds is who you need to see if you have questions and I'm not around."

"Or you could ask me," Robert volunteered, earning a glare from Jack. "I'd be happy to help with any questions. Or to give a tour of the grounds."

Glancing toward Jack first, Taylor smiled at Duffy and ignored Robert's comment. "Nice to meet you."

Once he'd shown her their "twenty-bed" operation, he asked, "You checked out the stages?"

She shook her head. "When I arrived, I went straight to the main medical tent, registered, then came here."

"You camping?"

She nodded. "Amy and I had planned to tent together with maybe a trip to her place for showers and refreshing ourselves if the shower lines were too long. I'm camping solo now."

"Don't let Robert hear you say that or he'll offer to share his tent."

Her gaze lifted. "He was just teasing."

"Don't you believe it," Jack warned. "You so much as give him a smile and he's going to be all over you in hopes of a festival fling. If that's not what you want, steer clear."

"Noted."

Jack eyed her a moment, waiting for her to elaborate or say something further. "Is that what you want, Taylor?"

"A fling with Robert?" She shook her head. "I came to spend time with my best friend, not to have a fling."

"That'll make my job of keeping you safe easier."

"He's dangerous?"

Feeling guilty he'd given her that impression, Jack shook his head. "No. Just making sure I keep my promise to Amy to watch out for you. She wouldn't be happy if I let someone break your heart while you're here."

"There is that," she agreed, studying him. Smiling, Taylor's eyes narrowed. "Why do I get the feeling you're way more dangerous than Robert ever thought of being?"

He laughed. Yep, she was onto him.

"Come on, let's walk around the grounds before it gets too crowded. People will be pouring in over the next twenty-four hours as this party gets started."

Taylor had to admit she was impressed at the organization of the event. There were three main stages and several smaller ones. The five-night event offered everything from big-name pop stars to small-time local bands hoping to make it big someday. There were huge rows of food vendors and a shopping village made up of tents offering their wares. There was a comedy tent, a dance party tent, sponsored by a popular music television station, and a dozen more entertainment tents. Some tents were huge commercial numbers with electricity and some having generator-run air-conditioners even. And people. People were everywhere.

"It already looks crowded," she mused, taking in the multitude checking out their surroundings prior to the first show kicking off. "How many more are expected?"

"They're expecting about a hundred thousand attendees. By this time tomorrow night this place will be packed."

Taylor nodded. She'd expected most of the festival-goers to be college-aged kids. Most were, but there was a huge variety of ages represented, even some young parents with two or three kids in tow and some who appeared to be older than Taylor's parents.

"Most of what we'll see in the medical tent will be dehydration and intoxication, but there's always a mix of other things thrown in just to keep things interesting."

Taylor knew security screened for drugs, but that where there was a will there was a way. Amy had told about some of the patients they'd seen over the years. Unfortunately, there had been a few overdose deaths.

"From what Amy's told me, boredom shouldn't be an issue."

He laughed. "Boredom is what I hope for at these events."

Taylor glanced his way. "Oh?"

"Boredom means everyone is having fun with no worries."

"Ah." Glancing out over the happy, energetic crowd, she nodded. "Then that's what I'm going to hope for, too. Boredom."

But glancing toward the man walking beside her, who was telling her about the different tents and upcoming acts as they made their way over to the main medical tent, Taylor suspected boredom was the last word she'd be using to describe the next few days.

CHAPTER TWO

TAYLOR FROWNED AT the pile of poles and canvas, then went back to studying the instructions. She was a highly skilled ICU nurse. She could put together a tent. No problem.

Well, okay, some problem.

Mainly, that every time she put one pole end in the designated loop it would pop out when she tried to put in the other end. What she needed was—

"You need help with that?"

Taylor jumped, then looked up at Jack. She started to tell him she had it, because she would figure it out and hadn't she made great strides in not depending on a man for anything?

But common sense won out, so she smiled and said, "Um…yeah, I do. I've got a tarp down for a moisture barrier, got my tent all spread out like these say…" she waved the instructions "…but that end doesn't want to stay in that loop thingy when I put in the other side."

Jack's lips twitched. "The loop thingy?"

Before she could say more, he bent down, threaded the pole back into the end loop just as she had. But when he bowed the pole and hooked the other side, the pole behaved and didn't slip out on the other end.

"Well," she mused, putting her hands on her hips, "you made that look easy."

"It's all in how you handle the pole."

Taylor's cheeks heated and she ordered her mind to get out of the gutter.

"Um...yeah...well..." She hemmed and hawed, then brushed her palms down her shorts. "Thank you for your help."

"Anytime."

His grin was cocky as all get-out. "Anything else I can help with?"

"I feel guilty you had to help with that," she admitted. A strong independent woman should have been able to figure out how to put up a tent, right?

"Wasn't any trouble. I was on my way to my tent to grab a drink."

"Your tent?"

He gestured to the tent next to hers.

Next to hers. Seriously? The medical staff parking/camping area located behind the main medical tent wasn't that big. What were the odds?

He was offering help, but that hard-won independent streak refused to be silent. "Grab that drink and check on me in a few minutes, if that's okay."

"Be glad to." His eyes danced with what she could only describe as happiness. How could any one man radiate so much positivity?

Trying to ignore the fact that Jack was a tent away, that if she coughed, sneezed, or made any other weird noises, he'd hear, Taylor pulled the air mattress from its box and placed it inside the tent. She hit the battery-operated control button and was relieved when the unit blew up perfectly. Within minutes she had her bed made and her bag to one side. The tent was large enough that both she and Amy could have set up their air mattresses, so with just the one she had floor space.

"Everything going okay?" Jack asked when she climbed out of the tent.

"So far," she told the man sitting in a fold-up chair facing in her direction.

He held a refillable drink container and a protein bar. "You know it's killing me not helping, right?"

"White knight syndrome?"

He shrugged. "Momma taught me to be useful syndrome."

Taylor laughed. "Fine. You can help."

Immediately he rose, set his water bottle down

on his much sturdier appearing table than the one she'd just pulled out of the back of her car.

"I take directions well."

Taylor arched her brow. "A man who takes directions well? I thought those were the things of unicorns and fairies."

He winked. "Try me and see."

Taylor gulped back the thoughts that ran through her mind. "Well, I've got to set up the canopy tent. Amy said to be sure to put it as close as possible so it would help shade my sleeping tent."

"Yep, otherwise your tent will be hot as Hades in the daytime."

She pulled out the canopy tent her friend had left in her living room along with the other camping items for Taylor to pick up on her way to the festival. "Let's see if we can figure this out."

The canopy tent was easier to set up, and not just because Jack was helping.

Well, maybe because he was helping. Certainly, it was more fun and had gone faster.

"What's next, ma'am?"

"The table?"

He lifted the folding table from where she'd propped it against her car and set it up beneath the canopy tent, which had been scooted partially over the entrance of the smaller tent she'd be sleeping in.

Holding up a lightweight tarp she'd pulled from a duffle bag that contained at least one more, Taylor said, "I found the tarp with the tent and used it as a moisture barrier per Amy's instructions, but was I supposed to do something with these?"

"Amy usually attaches them to the sides of the canopy to create shade and keeps one to put over her tent if the weather doesn't co-operate and it decides to flood."

Taylor wrinkled her nose. "If it decides to flood, I'll be sleeping in my car."

Jack laughed. "You wouldn't be the first person to do so. Just set an alarm so you don't overheat after the sun comes up. It gets too hot fast inside a vehicle." He took one of the tarps and began attaching it to the canopy. "With Amy canceling, I'm surprised you decided to camp rather than stay at her place."

Trying to mimic how he was hanging the tarp, Taylor began attaching a second tarp to another side. "She insisted that rather than go back to her place I stay here and enjoy my first music festival."

"Really?" He looked incredulous. "This is your first music festival?"

"Hard to believe I've been missing out on this

all these years." Giving him a wry look, she spread her arms to indicate the festival just beyond the main medical area.

Together they worked to attach the third tarp, leaving the fourth side open. "Since this is your first music festival experience, I'll make sure it's a good one so you'll want to come back."

Butterflies danced in Taylor's belly. "Oh?"

"Since neither of us are on duty tonight, you want to watch the shows with me?"

Ha. Was this a trick question or what? Wander around by herself or sit next to a charismatic man who had awakened her dormant hormones? Hmm...hard decision.

It should have been a harder decision given his profession.

Still, she was smiling when she said, "I'd love to."

Taylor could get into music festivals. Or maybe it was the man beside her she was into. Glancing over at him, she couldn't help but think how fortunate she was to have him there this week since Amy hadn't been able to attend. Otherwise she might really have packed up and gone to Amy's.

Amy had texted earlier to make sure she'd arrived, and everything was okay. She'd not mentioned her unexpected reaction to Jack but had said everything was great.

Maybe if Jack were anything other than a doctor, she'd give in to the heat, let herself have a free pass life experience.

She wrapped her arms around her knees and looked back toward the stage where a band with a current chart-topping song had kicked off the festival an hour before and was still jamming out.

Around them others on blankets were watching the show and others danced along to the tunes, some dressed similar to Taylor's shorts and T-shirt, some in costumes, some in not much of anything at all.

"Having fun?"

She smiled at Jack and nodded.

"The band is awesome, isn't it?"

Again, she nodded. She didn't really follow any particular band, but did enjoy singing along with the radio from time to time. The band playing really was good.

When the group on the main stage finished, Jack turned to her. "You want to stay here until the next band, move to a different stage, or go find something to eat?"

Her stomach growled. "Eat?"

He packed up the blanket they'd been sitting on into a backpack that he slung over his right shoulder. "What are you hungry for?"

"What are my options?"

"Anything from burgers to a meat and three. There seems to be vendors who offer just about anything you can think of. Why don't we walk around for a while and see if anything catches your eye?"

"Or my nose," she added, taking a sniff of the air. Something sure smelled good.

He laughed. "Or that."

They ended up getting bowls of jambalaya from a Cajun food booth and standing at one of the chest-high tables set up near the row of vendors.

"This is good," she enthused, hoping she didn't have food on her face or between her teeth.

He'd already finished his. "Yep."

Feeling self-conscious under his watchful eye, she asked, "Are there any particular bands you're hoping to catch tonight?"

He named one she'd heard of but couldn't recall the names of any of their songs. Sadly, she felt as if she'd been living under a rock since graduation. Before that, even.

She had been. She'd gone from toeing the line for her strict parents to toeing the line for Neil. She'd spent the last year learning to make decisions for herself, learning she didn't need to have anyone's directions or approval for the choices she made. If she messed up, so what? It was her life to live.

"That okay with you?"

She nodded. "Sounds good."

"If there are any particular shows you want to see, speak up and we'll go. I'm game for whatever."

"Duly noted." Game for whatever. He had no clue as to what ran through her mind at his innocent comment.

Or maybe, with the way his eyes danced, his comment hadn't been so innocent.

"How is it you've never been to a music festival?" He leaned across the table to stare into her eyes and, again, she wondered if perhaps he'd read her mind and knew more than she thought.

She shrugged. "Just not that lucky, I guess."

"I'm glad you're at this one."

"Me, too."

His grin shined brighter than the sparkly dance ball a few hundred yards away and Taylor really was glad she'd agreed to work the festival, that she'd gotten away from Louisville, and that she'd met Jack.

Because she was in charge of her life now, was making changes, reaching for new adventures, taking chances, had given herself permission to make mistakes as long as they were mistakes she'd chosen to make.

Her gaze connected with Jack's, her heart speeding up as she wondered if she'd choose Jack as her next new adventure. If she could give herself permission to take a chance that he'd be her next mistake.

Because becoming involved with a man, any man, would be a mistake.

Becoming involved with Jack would be a big one. Colossal.

Taylor didn't sleep well that night. Not that her bed wasn't semi-comfortable. It had been. The night air wasn't nearly as sticky and hot as she'd expected either. The temperature had almost been cool.

What had kept her awake had been the noises around the festival. Obviously, she and Jack had been the only people in the entire place who had wanted to sleep. Then again, there weren't that many inside the event grounds who would be getting up at four a.m. to go to "work" either.

Donning a pair of khaki shorts and a T-shirt, she pulled her hair up into a ponytail, then slipped out of her tent.

Her gaze immediately went to Jack's tent. In the dim moonlight and lights coming from the festival, she could see he was up. He gave a little wave.

Taylor's stomach grumbled. Whatever Jack

had going on his portable stove smelled a lot more mouth-watering than the breakfast bar with which she had planned to start her day.

"I made extra," he told her in a low whisper.

Although there was noise coming from beyond the other side of the main medical tent, the medical staff camping area itself was relatively quiet other than crickets chirping and the early morning crew slowly making their way out of their tents.

"Thanks," she mouthed, taking the plate. "Hey, this is good."

He grinned. "Did you think it would taste bad?"

She shook her head. "Smelled too good for that. Just wasn't expecting it to be amazing."

They finished up, cleaned up their mess, then headed to the main medical tent. When they got inside, they checked in, were given that day's mandatory medical staff T-shirt and would change each day. Guys changed T-shirts in the main area. Taylor fought—and lost—to keep her eyes from soaking up the rippling of Jack's muscles. As he pulled his T-shirt down over his six-pack, his gaze met hers and he grinned, as if he knew she'd been watching him and had liked what she'd seen.

"I, uh, need to put this on," she mumbled, turning to go to one of several enclosed areas in the tent where any private examinations would take place inside the main medical tent. She quickly stripped off her T-shirt and replaced it with the designated one.

She crammed her removed shirt into the backpack she'd brought with her and returned to where the others were waiting for a staff member to drive them to the medical tent.

When they arrived, Jack reached up to take Taylor's hand to assist her off the golf cart. It might have been before the crack of dawn, but that didn't stop the zings that shot up Taylor's arm at holding his hand. Zings shot and her heart kaboomed.

"Thank you," she murmured, cramming her fingers in her pocket the moment he let go. How was it possible to go from completely dead inside to so very aware? Had her body just saved years' worth of sexual nothingness and was unleashing it all at once?

And why, why, why, why couldn't he have been anything other than a doctor? To give in to Jack's smile would mean ignoring not only her man aversion but also her decision that never ever would she get involved with another doctor.

At the medical tent they switched with the night shift and took over the few cases currently being treated. Taylor reviewed a case of possible food poisoning and an intoxication patient.

As the sun came up and the hours passed, the temperature soared. A steady trickle of people came in with various complaints.

Two young girls came into the tent. One asked for a bandage for her leg as she'd tripped and skinned her knee.

Taylor started to register the girl and do minor wound care, but Duffy waved her off. "I've got this one."

While Duffy was cleaning the girl's grazed leg, another two young women came in. One was almost completely supporting the other.

"She started passing out but never completely did, but she's talking out of her head, like she did something, you know, but she didn't do anything," the patient's friend gushed, not pausing for breath as Taylor helped them over to a vacant cot.

"I was flipping out," the woman continued. "I wasn't sure she was going to make it here and then what was I going to do?"

"I'm just really hot," the barely coherent patient said, her hand on her temple. "And my head hurts."

"Name?"

"Cindy Frazier," the friend answered. "We're nineteen. I'm Lori. We're from Maine."

Maine? That was a long way to travel for a

music festival, Taylor thought as she got Cindy registered.

Taylor ran a thermometer over her forehead.

Eek. One hundred and five degrees Fahrenheit.

She glanced around to see who was free and could grab an ice pack. Everyone was with someone except Jack.

"Dr. Morgan?"

Odd to call him that when in her head he was Jack. He glanced up from his clipboard, his blue gaze meeting hers.

"I have a hyperthermia case. Temp is one-oh-five. Can you grab an ice pack and ice water, please, while I finish checking vitals?" She supposed she should have offered to get them and let him take over with the patient, but Jack didn't balk, just rushed to get the needed supplies.

Cindy moaned and clutched at her stomach.

"Are you feeling nauseous?"

Eyes squished closed, she nodded. "I may throw up."

Jack stepped up, handed Taylor the items she'd requested. "I'll get an emesis pan and anti-emetic."

Taylor wrapped the ice pack collar around the girl's neck.

"That's cold!" she complained, shivering.

"We have to cool you down. You got too hot

and you're dehydrated, that's why you're feeling so bad."

Jack was back, and handed the plastic pan to the girl. He bent to shine a penlight into Cindy's eyes, then her nose and mouth. He listened to her heart and lung sounds.

"She's tachycardic."

Taylor opened the bottle top then handed the girl the iced water. "I want you to get as much fluid in you as you can."

"I'll throw it up."

"Maybe not, but if you do, use the pan if you can. Just drink." She glanced at Jack. "You okay with me starting the cold IV fluid and putting the anti-emetic in?"

"You took the words out of my mouth."

She checked the girl's veins and frowned. Dehydrated, Cindy's veins were poor at best. Still, Taylor had always prided herself on being good at accessing veins and hopefully would hit her mark the first try, despite not having much to work with.

Gathering her supplies, Taylor then cleaned her IV site with an alcohol pad while Jack finished examining Cindy, including rechecking her temperature.

"Still one-oh-five."

"Is that bad?" Lori asked, wringing her hands as she watched them work on her friend.

"It hasn't gone up, so that's a good thing," Taylor assured her, breathing a sigh of relief when the IV catheter slid into Cindy's vein perfectly. "Once we get these cold fluids in, her temp should drop."

If not, they'd put her in the ice tub.

"I feel like I can't breathe," Cindy gasped, putting her hand to her chest.

"It's going to be okay, Cindy." Jack sounded calm as he continued to assess the girl, watching her closely. "Just take slow, deep breaths."

Cindy visibly took a deep breath.

As Taylor taped the IV line to Cindy's left hand, she fought breathing deeply herself as Jack's voice was so hypnotic.

"Your temperature will start dropping any minute," Jack assured their patient. "Once that happens, you'll slowly start feeling better."

Jack's soothing voice made Taylor feel better as she grabbed the anti-emetic to go into the IV. Lots better. How could he be so calm when the girl's situation really could turn dire if what they were doing didn't work?

"I'm scared," Cindy admitted, bursting into tears, which caused her friend to also burst into tears.

"Look at me, Cindy."

The young woman lifted her tearful gaze to Jack's. He took her hand in his and gave it a squeeze. "It's okay. You're okay. We're doing all the right things to get your temperature down and we'll keep you here until you're feeling okay. You're going to be fine."

"Phew," Lori sighed in relief, sniffling as she plopped down onto an empty cot next to Cindy's. "She's not the only one who's scared. I've heard about people dying at music events but never thought about it possibly happening to someone I knew. She had me terrified when she started blacking out."

Taylor leaned forward to inject the medication, but before she could administer it, Cindy's body tensed. Taylor grabbed for the emesis pan, but lightning fast Jack had it to the woman's mouth, making it just in time.

"Oh, no," her friend groaned as Cindy heaved her stomach contents into the pan. "This is bad. I know it is."

"It's not uncommon for someone with hyperthermia to throw up." Taylor injected the anti-emetic into the IV solution. "The nausea should calm down soon, too."

Fortunately, it did.

Due to the degree of Cindy's hyperthermia, Taylor stayed with her, closely monitoring her vitals over the next thirty minutes.

Jack came and went as he checked other patients who'd come in for care. Most were minor issues, thank goodness.

As Taylor checked Cindy's temperature yet again, Jack walked up behind her.

"What is her temp now?"

"Ninety-nine."

"That's awesome," Jack praised, placing his hand on Taylor's shoulder. "Almost back to normal."

Relieved at how Cindy was responding to their treatment and wondering at how her own temperature had just spiked at Jack's innocent touch, Taylor nodded.

He gave her shoulder a squeeze before his hand fell away.

Gracious. Had he felt it, too? The sparks that flew when they touched? Or was she just crazy and imagining things in the midst of patient care?

Cindy finished off her water.

Reaching to take the bottle, Taylor gave a thumbs-up. "Want another?"

Although her color and disposition had greatly improved, the girl still looked weak. "Will it help me get back to normal quicker?"

"You may not feel yourself for a few days but, yes, hydrating well is vital," Jack answered, then listened to Cindy's chest again. When he removed his stethoscope from his ears, he grinned. "Heart rate is down to eighty-eight."

"Is that good?" Lori asked. To give the girl credit, she'd stayed by her friend's side, encouraging her to drink more water and holding her hand during the times Cindy got overly emotional.

Taylor chatted with Cindy for a few minutes, then left her to rest on the cot with Lori watching over her so she could help with other patients now that Cindy was stable.

"Great job there," Jack praised when she joined him at a triage table, where he was attending to a new patient.

"Thanks. I'll take this one from here so you can check on the other patients," she offered, knowing the tent was hopping with patients who probably needed his attention.

Their gazes met. Taylor's belly flip-flopped.

Jack rose from where he sat. "Thanks."

The new patient looked worn out, hot and couldn't give any specific symptoms, just that she felt exhausted. Taylor took her information, checked her vitals—all of which were normal—then put her on a cot and went to get her water.

When she got back, the girl was sound asleep.

"Well, okay, then," she said, picking up the clipboard with the girl's information and making a note.

"We'll have some who do that." Jack walked up beside her to watch the girl sleep. "They'll come to medical just to take a break from the hyper-stimulation and to cool down."

"It's a whole different world from anything I've ever known," Taylor admitted.

"Just wait until we watch the shows tonight. Last night will seem tame."

She shot a curious look his way. He planned on them going to watch the shows together again?

"The costumes, the people, the vibe in the air." His excitement came through, creating its own vibe. "Tonight people will have found their bearings and will be more relaxed. There will be more booze, drugs, sex, more everything."

More. Her cheeks heated. "Oh."

"No worries. Most are here to have a good time. We're here to make sure they do it without any lasting problems."

His grin was so infectious Taylor's breath caught.

Apparently, it didn't matter that Jack was a doctor and she'd sworn the profession and men off forever.

Now that her body had remembered it was young, healthy, full of hormones, it refused to be ignored.

Not only refused to be ignored but demanded attention. Jack's attention.

Why not? an inner voice asked. It wasn't as if anything that happened this week would go beyond the music festival.

Maybe she could—should—forget an outside world existed and just go with the flow. Wasn't that what she was trying to do? Step outside her comfort zone?

Jack Morgan was way outside her comfort zone and would be one humdinger of a life experience.

CHAPTER THREE

BATHING HAD NEVER felt so good.

Taylor had had to wait in line over half an hour to get into the shower, but the wait had been worth it. To have washed the dust from her hair and put on clean clothes felt amazing.

When she went back to the medical camping ground, Jack, Duffy, Robert and a few others were playing guitars in front of Jack's tent. Duffy was singing a country song about wild women and drinking too much.

Taylor grabbed her chair and joined the group. Listening to their song, she brushed out her hair, then braided it into a French braid, twisting a band around the end. When she'd finished, her gaze collided with Jack's.

He'd been watching her. With more than casual interest.

Then again, there was nothing casual about the sparks that had flown between them all day.

He winked and, heart kerthunking, she winked back.

Something she'd never done. Her ex hadn't been the kind of man one winked at. Neil hadn't been playful or fun. Ever.

Jack was playful and fun.

At some point he'd gotten a shower, too. He looked refreshed in his navy shorts and T-shirt while he plucked the strings of a rather beat-up, well-loved-appearing guitar, keeping perfect tune with the others.

Having no musical talent, Taylor was impressed.

She was even more impressed when Duffy's song ended and they started playing another. This time Jack did the vocals. His voice was a raspy baritone that reached inside and tugged at her very being.

The man had a beautiful, unique timbre.

A beautiful, unique everything.

She wanted to close her eyes and just listen to his voice, but her eyes refused to be denied the privilege of feasting on the image of him strumming along on his guitar while he sang.

When the song ended, Taylor clapped and gave a self-conscious whistle. Another first. This stepping outside one's comfort zone thing wasn't so bad.

Actually, it was kind of fun.

"I think you have a groupie," Duffy teased.

"Never had a groupie before," Jack mused, his

smile aimed at Taylor. "But we are at a music festival, so I'm game."

"Can't say I've ever been a groupie," Taylor admitted, knowing her cheeks were pink but that a silly smile was on her face. "Maybe I'll settle for being an avid fan, rather than a full-fledged groupie."

"Far less fun. Stick with the groupie," Robert suggested, gathering a few laughs.

"Avid fan is more my speed," Taylor admitted, feeling a little self-conscious that all the men's attention was now on her rather than their music. "Don't stop playing on my account. I was enjoying listening."

"You play?" Duffy asked, offering her his guitar.

She shook her head. Maybe she'd add guitar lessons to the growing list of things she'd tried since her divorce. So far she'd taken art classes, cooking classes, exercise classes, and was taking a foreign language course online. Not necessarily to expand her horizons but to figure out things she liked and enjoyed rather than be an extension of her parents, then Neil.

"You sing?" Robert asked.

She gave him a dubious look. "Not if I want to keep any of you as friends."

A few chuckles sounded.

"We're not a picky crowd, so feel free to join in at any time. The more the merrier."

Duffy launched into another song, but Taylor didn't know the words so joining in wasn't an option even if she'd wanted to give it a try.

After a few more songs Robert stood, stretched, and announced he had plans to meet a cute little nurse who was working in the main medical tent. The others left one by one, leaving Taylor and Jack.

"Do you really not play or sing or you just didn't want to show up us guys?"

"Ha," Taylor snorted. "Believe me when I say I did you a favor by keeping my mouth shut."

Jack's gaze dropped to her lips. "A shame. I'm positive I'd enjoy hearing you sing."

"You only say that because you've not heard me do so," she assured him, thinking she'd never be comfortable enough to sing in public.

"You don't sing, you don't play music, and this is your first music festival." His gaze searched hers. "What do you do in your free time, Taylor?"

Good question. One that two years ago she'd have answered with do everything she could to keep her husband happy, spend all her time trying to somehow be good enough so that perhaps their failing marriage would morph into what she'd once dreamed it would be. A year ago she'd have answered with cry and try not to dwell on the mess she'd made by not really knowing the man she'd married in a whirlwind while thinking she was the luckiest girl alive that a handsome plastic surgeon wanted to marry a plain Jane like her.

Thank goodness she'd never given in to his wanting her to not work but stay home. As his wife, she'd gone part time, but had kept working. The ICU, her patients had been her solace. Other than her work, she'd had no life, no being Taylor, just Mrs. Dr. Neil Norris.

"I run." One of the habits she'd picked up immediately following her divorce.

"Competitively?"

She snickered. "Hardly. I run for me, to relieve stress, for exercise, to clear my head."

She'd started on a whim of wanting to be healthy but running had quickly become her therapy. She spent the time working through the past, how it had molded her, how she was determined to break those molds and forge herself into a person she liked. Neither her indifferent parents nor Neil got the final say on who she was.

"So you work, sleep and run." Jack frowned. "Not a very exciting life you're describing, Taylor. Surely there's more?"

"I never claimed I led an exciting life." She crossed her arms as she stared back.

"What else, Taylor?" he pushed.

Glancing down at the green grass beneath her tennis shoes, she shrugged. "I have all the usual hobbies people have." She did. Now. "I sculpt."

She'd signed up for the sculpting class after seeing an ad she'd come across on social media but had loved it from the first moment she'd felt the clay between her fingers.

Jack's brow lifted. "As in statues of naked men?"

Taylor rolled her eyes. "That's such a guy question."

His lips twitched. "But is it true?"

"A couple of times," she admitted, her face warm and getting warmer at how his eyes twinkled.

"In the name of art, right?" he teased.

Smiling, Taylor didn't bother to explain she'd been oblivious to the men who'd posed during her art class. She could barely recall what they'd looked like. What she'd enjoyed had been the feel of the clay beneath her fingers as she'd taken nothing and transformed it into something.

Much as she'd done with her life.

Nothing to something.

"I'd like to see some of your work."

Unless he saw the piece she'd brought to

give to Amy, it was unlikely. Until recently, she hadn't wanted anyone to see her work as too much of her was caught up in it.

"Or if you got the urge to work while here and needed inspiration..." His tone teased.

Yeah, had Jack been the model, she seriously doubted she'd have been oblivious. Looking at the man was like looking at the most interesting piece of artwork she'd ever encountered, beautiful, intriguing, and full of character.

Meeting his gaze and feigning excitement, she couldn't resist saying, "You really think Robert would do that for me?"

Jack laughed. "I'm sure you could convince him."

"I don't know," she said, trying to sound unsure. "There's that nurse he was meeting when he took off earlier."

"There is that." Jack's gaze stayed locked with hers, both of them smiling, Taylor feeling really good on the inside.

This, she thought. This was fun. Light and held no real meaning. Just a man, a woman, and good old-fashioned physical chemistry.

Was the new Taylor the real Taylor, okay with starting something with Jack—a doctor, for goodness' sake!—when she knew they'd go their separate ways when the music festival ended because she didn't want a relationship?

Not that she suspected he did either, just that she didn't want a man in her life. She had too many things to still learn about herself.

"Hungry?"

Starved, and not for food. She wanted what she saw in his eyes, in what being near him hinted at within her body.

Did that mean she was okay with a meaningless fling?

Or maybe she just wanted to learn what Jack could teach her about herself?

He propped his guitar against his chair and stood. "I have sandwich stuff. You want to eat with me or grab something from a vendor?"

"You don't have to feed me." Was she talking food or sex? Or both? "I brought food."

His lips twitched. "Something more exciting than ham and cheese?"

"Does such a thing exist?" she asked with feigned seriousness, eliciting a laugh.

While he pulled out his sandwich supplies from his cooler, Taylor dug through her supplies to find a plastic container of cookies she'd made, thinking she and Amy would gobble them up.

When she set them on his table, he stopped what he was doing and helped himself to one.

"Hey, these are good."

He sounded so surprised that Taylor laughed.

"You didn't mention anything about being a good cook," he accused.

"I'm not, but I can bake cookies."

During her classes, she'd discovered she found cooking so-so but enjoyed baking. She'd mastered basic skills but had thrown herself into spending more time at her sculpting class.

"They're good," he repeated, reaching for another.

She slapped at his hand. "Didn't your mother make you wait until after dinner before having dessert?"

His gaze lifted to hers and, grinning, he shook his head. "My mom would have been the first to encourage me to have the good stuff first because life is short."

Taylor's brow rose. Wow. "Sounds fun."

And very unlike her older parents who hadn't planned to have children, hadn't wanted them, but had been stuck with her all the same.

"But not very nutritious," Jack added wryly.

"There is that."

Jack spread a blanket on the ground a good distance back from the stage. He and Taylor could have made their way closer, but closer to the stage meant more crowded. No way could they have seen from their sitting positions.

Taylor's arms were wrapped around her knees

and she was watching the band as if they were the most fascinating group she'd ever seen. Her head bobbed ever so slightly to the beat.

"Our little jam session may fail to impress you now that you've seen this."

She glanced toward him. "Not likely. You were good."

"Glad you thought so."

Still looking his way, she asked, "Did you ever want to play music professionally?"

He chuckled. "Probably the same as every other kid who played an instrument dreams of being a rock star. But if you mean was I ever in a band then, yeah, a few over the years."

"What happened?"

"I wasn't that good, and I fell in love with medicine."

Her expression became thoughtful. "A musician or a physician. Interesting choices."

"Maybe if I'd been better at the music there wouldn't have been a choice." He shrugged. "Once I was exposed to medicine, there wasn't a choice. I knew that's what I was supposed to do."

Not once had he ever regretted that decision. Sometimes life threw things at you to point you in the right direction. In his case, life had hit him over the head—heart—to steer him down the right path.

"I'm glad you get to play from time to time and have both in your life."

Ready to shove the past back as far away as it would go, he took a drink. "I enjoy life."

A true statement. He'd dealt with what had happened years ago to Courtney and had spent years making atonement. It was all he could do.

"Not many people can say that," Taylor mused, her voice sounding almost wistful.

He turned toward her. "Can you?"

She took a long time answering, but finally nodded. "I am enjoying life very much. Thank you."

The emotion in her voice, almost surprise, at her answer did funny things to Jack's chest.

He reached over, took her hand into his and gave a reassuring squeeze. "I'm glad you're enjoying life, Taylor."

He was also glad that rather than pull her hand away, she laced her fingers with his and shot a grateful smile toward him. As if maybe she'd meant right now, this very moment, was what had made her say she was enjoying life.

That he played a role in her happiness.

A humbling thought.

There was something fragile about Taylor. Something that brought out a protectiveness that left him feeling a bit lost.

In the past, if he'd felt an attraction to a woman

and that attraction was reciprocated, he'd acted without hesitation. Lord knew, he was no saint. Far, far from it.

Taylor felt an attraction to him. He was sure of it. Although there was a hesitation on her face at times, she hadn't really tried to hide her interest. But there was a vulnerability in her eyes that had him second-guessing himself. He didn't do vulnerable in his personal relationships and sure didn't want to feel protective of someone he was destined to walk away from.

Still, what he wanted to do was lean over and kiss Taylor.

They wouldn't be the only couple at the concert making out. Kissing would be tame compared to some of the amorous sessions that happened around the festival.

But most of those making-out sessions were just chemistry playing out between young, healthy couples.

Just?

What was it he thought was between Taylor and him should he kiss her, if not *just* chemistry?

He didn't do relationships that weren't just physical chemistry. Not ever.

Well, once, but never again.

CHAPTER FOUR

IT HAD BEEN a long time since Taylor had been on a date.

Years.

The last dates she'd been on had been with Neil.

Neil, who had been perfectly put together, clothes always perfectly arrayed and wrinkle free, appearance always perfectly groomed, hair always perfectly styled.

Neil, who had always taken her to the nicest restaurants, to premier shows in Louisville, to only the best of the best. Taylor had taken that to be a sign of him trying to impress her. In reality, it had only been Neil being Neil and wanting to show off his possessions to the world. He thought *he* deserved the best of the best, that the entire world revolved around him.

She'd been the envy of her fellow nursing students because the hospital's most eligible bachelor was besotted with her, bought her clothes and jewelry to wear to events with him. If only they'd known the only person Neil had been besotted with was himself.

She still wasn't sure what had attracted Neil to her. He'd wanted to change everything about her. Maybe he'd wanted a doll to bend and shape into what he wanted her to be. She'd played that role well for her parents. Letting him take over had been easy. When he'd decided she was who he'd wanted for a wife, she'd thought she was the luckiest girl alive. Plain her the wife of a renowned plastic surgeon who wanted to give her things and show her off to the world.

They'd been the envy of all their friends—Neil's true purpose.

To Neil, she'd been a possession. A piece added to his collection to be seen and not heard. Had she not caught him cheating, she might still be in her oblivious bubble of living her life on eggshells.

"Whatever you're thinking, stop."

Taylor glanced toward the man next to her. A man who was wearing shorts and a T-shirt, and whose pulled-back long hair was unkempt in a sexy sort of way—a man who had a shadow on his face where he needed to shave, and whose blue eyes were fringed with thick, dark lashes.

A man who made her stomach flip-flop. Jack seemed comfortable with who he was and didn't need to impress anyone.

Which felt like a breath of fresh air.

"Deal," she agreed, inhaling deeply, determined she would push thoughts of Neil far from her mind. These days, she rarely thought of him, but meeting Jack seemed to have triggered a plethora of comparisons.

"Good." Jack studied her. "I was beginning to think I was going to have to visit medical for crush injuries. Quite a grip you have there."

Relaxing her hold, Taylor glanced at where their fingers were interlaced. She liked his hands. Strong, capable, clean but not professionally manicured and softer than hers. Had she been clamping down or holding on for dear life?

She glanced back up. "Sorry."

Eyes locked with hers, he lifted her hand to his lips and pressed a kiss against her fingers. "You're forgiven."

Taylor's stomach bypassed flip-flops and went into full out Olympian gymnast gold medal mode. Wow. If she'd thought his touch caused zings, his lips were powerhouses.

"That was easy," she pointed out, wondering why she was tempting fate. "Not making me beg for forgiveness?"

Neil would have made her grovel.

Ugh. She didn't want to keep comparing Jack to Neil, but perhaps it was inevitable.

Jack's eyes were locked with hers, his expression serious, his hand warm around hers. "Forgiveness isn't on the list of things I want you to ever beg me for."

Taylor's insides quivered. She swallowed the lump in her throat and turned back toward the stage and pretended to watch the band.

All her brain could process was that Jack had kissed her fingers, had implied he'd like her to beg him for…for what?

Sex.

If she was willing, he wouldn't make her beg.

Heaviness plagued her chest, making breathing difficult.

She'd been over-the-moon giddy that her body wanted him, but the reality was she'd only had sex with one man and she'd been married to him.

Maybe that's why Neil had married her.

Because she'd refused to sleep with him, saying she was saving herself for marriage. His ego had liked it that he'd been the only man she'd been with. Or maybe it was the challenge of possessing what he'd been denied.

"What's his name?"

"Who?" she asked, glancing toward Jack.

"The man you keep thinking about."

She winced. Obviously, she sucked at hiding her emotions. "I'm sorry."

"Your thoughts aren't good ones."

She glanced down at their hands. "Was I

squeezing your fingers again? Sorry." She lifted her gaze to his. "I'd never intentionally hurt you."

He gave her hand a gentle squeeze. "Despite the fact we just met, I know that about you."

"How?" she asked, her voice catching in her throat and coming out hoarse.

"The same way you know I'd never intentionally hurt you."

She nodded. Which was crazy. She didn't know him, and you'd think she knew better than to ever trust a man again.

Perhaps it was because he was Amy's friend, but she believed the cause ran deeper.

Restlessness overtook her and she needed to move.

"Can we walk for a bit?" She stood, brushed off her shorts. "I need to move."

As the band was still playing, surprise darkened the blue of his eyes. "Then we'll move."

He shook out their blanket, put it in his backpack, and took her hand back into his. They walked in silence, making their way through the crowd. When they reached the fence along one edge of the festival grounds they turned and made their way back toward the stages. The show they'd been watching had finished and the crowd was thinning to head to one of the smaller stages.

"Sorry I made you miss the last of the show."

"Not a problem. I'd rather have been with you."

"Yeah, right," she snorted.

"Really."

She glanced toward him, saw genuine concern on his face. "Thank you."

"For?"

"Being so nice."

One corner of his mouth tugged upward, digging a dimple into his cheek. "Well, I did promise Amy to take care of you and make sure you had a good time."

Taylor stopped walking. "Is that what this is?"

"This?" He looked confused.

She lifted their raised hands.

An odd noise, almost a snort, came from deep in his throat. "Amy is a good friend, but I wouldn't become romantically involved with someone for her sake."

He shook his head as if to clear the very idea from his mind.

Taylor arched her brow. "Romantically involved?"

A repentant sort of grin on his face, he shrugged. "I guess that was presumptuous."

"Is that what's happening here?" she pressed, needing to hear him verbally confirm what was happening. "Us becoming romantically involved?"

He searched her gaze. "You tell me. Is that what you want?"

Refusing to look away, she held his gaze, determined to make sure he understood who her core being was. "I don't sleep around."

Sex, or even thinking about sex, just hadn't been an issue until she'd met Jack. She'd not really thought about or tried to figure out what she, the Taylor she was morphing into, wanted regarding a sex life because she'd thought she wouldn't have to deal with that until way into the future.

"Good," he said. "Neither do I."

"No, I mean I really don't." She paused, tried to figure out how to explain, feeling it imperative she make him understand. "It makes me old-fashioned, but the only person I've been with is my husband."

At Jack's look of surprise, she corrected, "My *ex*-husband."

His expression softened. "That you haven't slept around isn't a negative in my book, Taylor."

"But you wouldn't be opposed to us having sex?"

One side of his mouth hiked up, revealing a gorgeous dimple. "Is that a trick question?"

His response shouldn't annoy her, but for some reason it did. She pulled her hand free. "I want an honest answer, Jack."

"I gave you one." His expression grew serious. "Besides, you knew the answer when you asked."

"How would I know?"

"You knew the moment you walked into the medical tent and our gazes met," he pointed out. "I instantly felt a connection and you felt it, too. If I'm mistaken, tell me."

Taylor couldn't believe they were having this conversation in the middle of a crowd. They'd stopped walking. People thronged all around them, yet no one was paying them the slightest attention.

"You aren't wrong," she admitted.

He gave a low laugh. "Is that easier than saying you want me, too?"

"Even if I did, it doesn't mean we're going to act on those feelings," she pointed out, even though she wondered if that's exactly what that meant. "I don't do that."

He didn't look upset at her answer, just asked, "Why not?"

Stunned, Taylor stared. "What do you mean?"

"Why don't you have sex?" he clarified.

Her face caught fire. She couldn't believe they were discussing her sex life—her lack of a sex life. "Because…"

"How long have you been divorced, Taylor?"

She'd told him the only man she'd been with

was her ex-husband, but something in his voice, his eyes said he knew more than what she'd revealed about her past. What had Amy told him? That Taylor had screwed up her life by marrying a man who had been all shiny surface and no depth? That she was lonely and desperate?

She wasn't. This past year had been about healing, finding Taylor, not about replacing Neil. She didn't want to replace Neil. Not when she'd finally started discovering who she was and liking the woman emerging. The adult Taylor who didn't have to abide by her parents' heavy hand or be under her ex-husband's critical thumb.

She'd fight to protect that Taylor, would go to great lengths to keep any man from changing who was emerging from the dark cocoon she'd been encased in her whole life.

"A little over a year."

"And you've not had sex during the past year? Not even a rebound fling?"

She'd only thought she'd felt hot before. Now she burned so brightly she was surprised everyone wasn't whipping out their sunglasses to protect their eyes.

"You don't have to answer. I can see it on your face. So again I'll ask, why haven't you had sex since your divorce? Are you still in love with him?"

"No." Unable to stand still, she took off walking, again, making her way through the throng of music lovers.

"Then why choose to be celibate?" Jack asked from beside her, obviously determined to finish their conversation.

"Not everyone has to go around having sex all the time, you know." She glanced his way.

His brow arched. "Is that what you think I do?"

"I don't know what you do. I just met you. Maybe you have a fling during every one of these music festivals and I'm just this festival's chosen partner."

"I haven't."

Why did his answer make her heart beat more wildly? Why did their conversation feel so important?

She tilted her chin higher. "But you have had flings?"

"Have I had mutually consensual and satisfying sex during a music festival?" Staring intently into her eyes, he nodded. "Yes. More than once. Is that what you want to hear, Taylor? That I have had a healthy, enjoyable sex life? Does my admission make me less in your eyes?"

Taylor realized they'd reached the other end of the festival grounds and were near the medical tent and the Oasis. The haven was practically deserted. Letting go of his hand, she took off running towards the Oasis and dropped down onto the sand.

The Oasis had called to her like some mystical mirage offering what she needed. For all her pushing, Jack hadn't raised his voice or seemed mad, more intent on pressing her to find answers within herself. As if he realized she needed those answers more than he did.

He didn't run after her but, hands in his shorts pockets, he strolled towards her, whistling a tune that sounded similar to one of the songs they'd listened to the band play earlier.

When he reached her, he didn't say anything, just sat down in the sand beside her, staring out toward the closest stage, and patiently waited for her to say something.

It was a long time before she found words. She marveled that he sat silently with her, giving her the time and space to get her thoughts together.

"One of the reasons I've not had sex in the past year is that I haven't *wanted* to have sex." She took a deep breath. "Not even a hint of wanting to touch or have sex." She exhaled. "Not until now." Another deep inhalation and exhalation because she might pass out if she didn't force herself to breathe. "You're the first person I've wanted to have sex with since my divorce, and I want you. A lot. I find that exciting and terrifying."

There. She'd said the words out loud. Let him think what he may.

"Is it wrong if I say I'm honored?"

His voice sounded so cocky and his eyes danced with such wicked pleasure that Taylor's hackles rose.

"Don't patronize me, Jack Morgan."

His eyes remaining locked with hers, he lifted her chin to make her look into his eyes.

"I want you, Taylor. A lot. More than a lot." The colored lights providing a soft glow around the oasis glittered in his eyes. "Hearing you say you want me too doesn't generate a single patronizing thought."

Staring into his eyes, seeing so much emotion reflected there, Taylor swallowed. "What does it do?"

"Makes me want to kiss you even more than I already did."

Jack wanted to kiss her.

She'd known that.

Still, his words thrilled her, made her want to jump up and down and dance around the sand-pit like a giddy schoolgirl.

His words also made her want to take off running again. As far as her feet would take her because Lord help her at the things his admission did to her insides.

"We just met yesterday," she reminded herself as much as him.

His gaze held hers. "I haven't forgotten."

Her heart slammed against her ribcage so hard that surely he felt the impact of each beat. "It's too soon."

His thumb stroked across her jawline. "I know."

But even as the words left his mouth she leaned over and brushed her lips against his.

Oh, heaven. His lips were soft.

And *electric*.

It was barely more than a peck before she pulled back, searched his eyes, making sure the pounding inside her body wasn't deafening him.

It was deafening her.

Had he felt the same pleasure at the touch?

His held fell away from her face and he started to say something, but rather than let him she pressed her mouth against his again. This time she deepened the kiss and kept her eyes locked with his in the faint glow of the colored lights.

Those lights must be why a brilliant kaleidoscope flashed through her mind.

His lips were warm, undemanding, and yet nothing had ever demanded so much from her.

The kiss drew out every nerve ending, reached every cell, refused to let any part of her be passive. Everything about him necessitated action.

He wasn't touching her anywhere except her lips, yet every part of her felt him. His eyes darkened to depths she wanted to topple into and drown within.

She knew she could push him away, could stand up and walk away, could tell him to stop at any point she wanted this to end, and he'd let her. She had entire control and the knowledge, the surety emboldened her to not do any of those things.

Instead, she got lost in the inky blueness that stared back, in the perfect pressure of his mouth against hers, tasting, caressing, tempting.

Jack wanted to kiss her.

He was kissing her.

She kissed him, not regretting that she'd leaned over and started this, but embracing this newly found freedom just as she'd embraced her body's initial reaction to him.

Jack made her come to life, awakening new and exciting parts of her she hadn't known existed.

Her heart raced, thundering like a stampeding herd. Her lungs struggled to get oxygen to her brain. She gave in to the escalating excitement at her core and kissed Jack with hunger.

With certainty.

Never had she felt so starved for what his lips gave.

Never had she felt the heat mounting inside her and pushing upward and outward.

Time faded. She had no idea how long they kissed, just that every breath she took was his, every sensation inside her started and ended with Jack.

Sweet, heavenly, laidback Jack who didn't mind giving her control of their kiss.

A group of teens came running onto the sand near them. Taylor pulled back.

Breathless, she stared at Jack in awe.

He grinned.

Amazed at the relief, the happiness that flooded her at his smile, she grinned back.

So that was what a first kiss should feel like.

Amazing and worthy of shooting stars and firework displays.

Jack made her feel good inside, made her feel alive, made her feel as if she was a whole woman, as if she knew exactly who she was and what she wanted from life.

She wanted to wrap her arms around herself and give herself a hug.

And maybe a high-five, too, that she'd kissed him and it had been perfect.

Holding hands, she and Jack went back to the main stage, spread their blanket, and watched the next act as if nothing monumental had happened between them. When the show finished they made their way to the medical staff camping area.

Taylor's heart kerthunked with each step they took into the campground, with each campsite they passed, drawing them nearer and nearer to theirs.

When they stood outside her tent, they paused, looked at each other, a thousand questions bouncing between them.

Jack's gaze glittered. "'Night, Taylor."

Disappointment hit that he wasn't planning to spend the night inside her tent.

She wanted him inside her tent.

Inside her. She wanted to loosen his hair from its band and run her fingers through his silky locks. She wanted so much.

So much it stunned her.

"'Night, Jack," she whispered back.

A smile still on his face, he winked, then closed the distance to his tent.

Taylor watched as he unzipped the flap, glanced her way one last time, then disappeared.

Part of her wanted to throw caution to the wind and follow him, but another part wasn't willing to risk ruining the best night she'd had in a long, long time.

Maybe ever.

CHAPTER FIVE

JACK'S GAZE DRIFTED to Taylor yet again. It was early morning. The sun was just starting to rise over the hundred-acre Tennessee farm where the festival took place each year. Soon they'd wake a few who had spent the night in the medical tent, not due to any emergency but who'd partied too much and had needed to sleep it off.

Jack never minded that. Part of their job was to provide a safe place for festival goers.

Like the young woman whom Taylor was currently settling into the cot. A couple of friends had dropped her off, saying she wasn't acting right. Most of the patients they saw weren't in any real danger, but there were always those few.

"Busy morning," Taylor mused as she handed him the clipboard with her notes.

Skimming what she'd written, he nodded. "Each night of the festival brings a few more than the night before as the heat, booze, and lack of sleep kick in."

"Guess it's a good thing we're off tomorrow, eh?" she teased.

"Are you planning to stay at the festival tonight or go back to Amy's apartment?"

The surprise in her eyes said she hadn't thought about leaving the festival.

"What am I asking? This is your first music festival. Of course you're staying. Awesome bands are scheduled for tonight."

"Um…right." She smiled. "You know me and music so you may have to point them out."

His lips twitched. "That mean you want to hang with me tonight?"

"Yes." Relief shone in her big brown eyes. "Would that be okay?"

He grinned. "I'd say it'd be pretty amazing."

Her eyes brightened, and she smiled at him as if he'd just told her she'd won the lottery.

Refocusing his mind on the fact he still had a whole lot of hours to get through on today's shift, he glanced over again at the clipboard she'd handed him. Looked pretty run of the mill.

"Anything I need to know about our latest?"

Taylor shook her head. "She'll likely be fine in a few hours. Duffy is talking with her now to see if she knows what she took. During triage, she told me she didn't take anything, but he has a way of getting the truth."

Jack nodded. He'd seen Duffy work his magic

first-hand. Unfortunately, there were times when a person didn't know they'd been slipped something, or they simply didn't know what they'd taken and no amount of talking could reveal it.

A long black-haired beauty flashed into his mind.

Sometimes the poison took hold and never let go.

He'd escaped.

Courtney hadn't…

Just as his eyes were about to close to the wave of pain her memory triggered, a young man to Jack's left began violently trembling on his cot. An emergency medical technician had been doing the heavily intoxicated patient's intake, along with another who'd brought him into the medical tent.

Jack and Taylor were immediately at his side.

"Has he been given Narcan?" Jack asked, noting the man's blue lips as he lifted the man's eyelids to check his pupils. Pinpoint and no tracking.

"I injected him within two minutes of his arrival. He seemed to be stabilizing, his respirations picking up a little, heart rate, too. Then this shaking started and he looks awful."

"Give him another dose," Jack ordered, wondering if his thoughts of Courtney had somehow conjured the young man's turn for the worse.

"Pulse is thready—about fifty," Taylor told him, propping the guy's legs up. "Respirations ten."

Hell.

Glancing toward Taylor, he motioned to their crash cart. "I may need to vent him. Have everything here, just in case. This kid isn't going to die on our watch."

But it seemed he was going to give it a try.

The EMT called for an ambulance while they worked. Jeff would be shipped to the local hospital for care.

Just as Taylor got back with the crash cart, the kid's respiration rate dropped further.

If they could just keep him alive...

When Jack turned to Taylor, he didn't have to say a thing. Like the great nurse he'd already discovered she was, she was ready, gloved him up, then gave him the intubation tube.

Intubating patients wasn't something he did a lot of at the events he worked, but he'd gotten a plethora of practice at the emergency room these past few months. The tube slid into place. Jack slid his stethoscope on, listened to make sure placement was correct as the man's chest rose and fell.

Glancing up at Taylor, he gave a thumbs-up.

* * *

"I feel as if I'm wearing half the farm."

Jack glanced at where Taylor sat on the golf cart. Strands of her hair had worked loose from her braid and flew about in the wind. A folded bandana covered the lower part of her face to save her from breathing in the dust kicked up from the golf cart. Dark glasses shielded her eyes from the bright sun. She wore the "Medical Staff" T-shirt she'd been given that morning and loose cuffed khaki shorts. A shiny sheen of sweat coated her skin, as did a layer of dust.

"So many jokes I could make," he teased, thinking she looked beautiful, if a bit tired. No wonder. The medical tent had been hell today. A total nightmare. Thank God it had calmed down about an hour prior to the end of their shift.

Taylor rolled her eyes. "You could, but should you?"

"Which is why I'll keep my farm jokes to myself."

"I appreciate that."

"You don't think you'd appreciate my farm humor?"

"Who knows? Maybe I would have even if they were *baa*-d."

He laughed at her play on farm humor.

"Either way, even if I have to wait in line hours to get a shower, I am taking one."

"Agreed." He was hot and sweaty himself. And somewhere between emotionally exhausted and exhilarated.

Today had been rough for more reasons than one. Which was why he normally didn't let the memory of Courtney into his head, ever.

Not that she was ever far away, it was just that he didn't consciously let thoughts of her take hold. Not like he had today.

"Wow. Don't you look as pretty as a Georgia peach?"

"Thank you." Taylor fought not to blush at Duffy's compliment. She wore a loose tie-dye sundress that tied around her neck and a pair of crisscrossed lace-up-her-legs sandals that she'd bought just for the weekend. For convenience's sake, she pulled her hair back up into its braid. Plus, her hair off her neck would be much cooler in the Tennessee heat. Because she was spending the evening with Jack, she'd brushed on a light coat of mascara and glossed her lips.

He didn't say anything, but his eyes told her he appreciated her efforts.

"You sure you aren't up for a festival fling?" Robert asked, his tone light, teasing. "A few whispered sweet nothings and you could steal me away from Amber."

"Yeah, yeah. You say that but I saw how you

were following her around like a besotted puppy earlier today," Taylor teased back, not feeling threatened by Robert in the slightest. Not after how she'd seen how kind he was during patient care. The man had a big heart.

Robert looked sheepish at her claim. "She is a pretty little thing, isn't she?"

Taylor agreed. She'd met Amber earlier in the day. The woman was a tiny powerhouse of a nurse with bright eyes and a brighter smile.

Taylor's gaze shifted back to Jack, who was watching her with those ethereal blue eyes. Despite the stressful day they'd had in the medical tent, he looked completely relaxed. He, Duffy, Robert, and a few others were sitting around. Jack's guitar was propped beside his chair so they'd probably been playing but were just chatting now.

While she put away her toiletries, Jack moved her chair for her to join them. The guys sat talking about past music festival adventures, trying to impress Taylor by upping each tale told. At one point her belly hurt from laughing so hard.

"The first gig I want to see starts at seven. You game still?" Jack asked, standing to put his guitar back in a beat-up case, then putting it in the passenger seat of his Jeep.

"I am," she agreed, conscious that the others were watching them. Ha. She imagined in this environment it wasn't difficult to pick up on romantic happenings during the festival.

Grabbing her sunglasses, a loose bag to toss over a shoulder, and a straw hat, she joined him and they headed into the main event area to find a spot as close to the stage as they could get and still spread their blanket.

"I'm surprised we haven't seen any injuries from people getting stepped on," she teased as they spread their blanket. Even though there was still a good forty-five minutes before show time, a crowd was already gathering.

He laughed. "You're right, but I don't recall having seen anyone with that particular complaint."

Once their blanket was spread, Jack offered to go and grab pizza and beer.

Taylor lay back, covered her face with her straw hat, and soaked up the late evening sunshine. It was hot, but not unbearably so. She must have dozed off because the next thing she knew Jack was back.

They ate, chatted, and Jack asked how she and Amy had become friends. By the time the show started, they were surrounded by festival goers.

Around them people were dancing and singing along. The band was one Taylor knew and soon, to her astonishment, she was singing along, too. Probably because the music was so loud no one could discern her voice over anyone else's anyway.

The group led into one of their most popular hits and the crowd went wild, cheering, screaming, and jumping up and down. Jack stood and held his hand out to her. Not sure what he intended, Taylor let him pull her to her feet.

The next thing she knew she was in front of him, dancing, his arm around her waist as they sang along with the band.

It might have been the beer. Or it might have been Jack's arms around her, but Taylor felt good.

Really, really good.

And free.

She'd never felt comfortable singing or dancing in front of others, but as she swayed to the beat and sang the words, she felt great.

The song ended, and another started. The crowd was really into the music and someone had started hitting a giant beach ball around.

When it bounced her way, Taylor tapped it back up into the air, thinking, *How fun.*

"Good hit," Jack praised, taking her hand into his then turning his attention back to the stage.

His hand holding hers stole all Taylor's attention.

Jack. That was the song she was interested in singing. In dancing to.

Jack.
Jack.
Jack.

He turned toward her and she realized she'd said his name out loud.

Caught up in the moment, she stretched forward and planted a kiss on his lips. A habit she seemed to be developing.

Surprise lit his eyes, then he grinned. "Enjoying yourself?"

"Immensely," she answered, then laughed and spun around. As she did so, a young man in his early twenties grabbed her hand, bowed, then spun her again.

Laughing, Taylor shrugged at Jack and let the man lead her in another spin, after which he handed her back to Jack and moved on to another nearby lady to do the same.

Taylor's gaze met Jack's. He was smiling. It struck her that Neil wouldn't have been. First off, she couldn't imagine him at a music festival. But if he had been and had witnessed her dance, he'd have accused her of flirting with the man, of egging on his attention. Despite her efforts to reassure him, she'd have paid the price for the young man's foolery.

Tension started tightening her neck muscles, but she shook it off. Neil was no longer in her life and never would be again. She wouldn't let him ruin the present or her future the way he'd tainted her past.

She squeezed Jack's hand. "Thank you."

Jack's brow lifted. "For?"

"Not being upset."

Genuine confusion shone on his face. "Why would I be upset?"

Exactly. He shouldn't have been.

Still holding her hand, he pulled her to him. "I want you to have a good time, Taylor."

"Because you promised Amy?"

"Amy who?" he teased, brushing his lips across her forehead.

Smiling from the inside out, Taylor laughed.

"Come on," he told her. "Let's dance."

They danced. And sang. And got caught up with the partying crowd around them. One band led into another.

Never in her life had Taylor let herself go and just let the music take over who she was and move her body. Never had she laughed so much, felt so much like she belonged to the beating rhythm of the crowd.

On a high, Taylor flopped down on their blanket and stared up at the night sky with awe and amazement at herself, at the music, at the fun crowd, at Jack.

Rolling over, she pulled her cellphone from her bag. "It's after midnight."

Lying down beside her, Jack asked, "You have somewhere you need to be?"

"Not particularly, but we've been up since before four this morning," she reminded him.

"You tired?"

"Maybe a little," she said, knowing he had to be exhausted. Just because she felt energized it didn't mean he wasn't tired. Not that he looked it but, still, she needed to be respectful of the fact that for him this wasn't all new and sparkly.

"Ready to go back to the campsite?" he asked.

She wasn't really, but logic said she should. "Whenever you are."

His gaze narrowed then he shook his head. "If you're up for it, we'll stick around for the next band."

It was almost three when they made it to their tents.

Taylor had wondered how they'd do this. If Jack would kiss her goodnight or if she'd kiss him again, and they'd go from there.

Other than when she'd kissed him earlier and his having kissed her forehead and hand a couple of times, they hadn't kissed, not really kissed, since the night before.

But rather than kiss her outside her tent, he squeezed her hand and whispered goodnight.

It had been, Taylor thought as she watched him go into his tent. A very good night.

The best night.

But it could have been better, a voice shouted in her mind.

It could have been a night where she invited Jack into her tent so she could kiss him as many times and ways as she wanted.

Because, despite her vow that she was fine without a man, she definitely wanted this one.

CHAPTER SIX

THE HEAT WOKE Taylor earlier than she'd planned. Using baby wipes, she cleaned the stickiness off her skin as best as she could, then climbed out of her tent.

"Good morning, Sleeping Beauty."

"Morning." She glanced toward Jack's tent, then smiled at the man who'd starred in her dreams. His hair was in its usual loosely pulled-back style. His T-shirt advertised a music festival she'd never heard of and his shorts were more colorful than her dress from the night before. He should look ridiculous, but instead he looked relaxed and gorgeous and perfect.

"Breakfast?" he offered. "I saved some."

She joined him beneath his canopy tent and took his offering. Eggs, bacon, and a couple of slices of buttered toast. The man knew how to camp.

"You're spoiling me."

"Gotta keep up your strength. We have a long day ahead of us."

Mouth full, she arched a brow.

"You're at a music festival, Taylor, and we don't work. As soon as you're through eating, we're going to go have fun."

"More fun than last night?" She hadn't thought there were any bands playing until late afternoon, but perhaps she'd been wrong.

"Way more."

It was hard to imagine recapturing the carefree abandon she'd experienced with him the night before. However, today was a new day and she was game for whatever he had planned for them.

All in the name of new adventures and life experiences, of course.

Taylor eyed the little sand-filled sack dubiously. "I'm not sure about this."

"It's easy once you get the hang of it." As if to prove his point, Jack kicked his foot up to his side and hit the small sack a few times.

Behind her shades, Taylor's eyes narrowed at the ball being kicked around. "Let's go have fun, you say," she intoned, knowing she was about to try something else she'd never done. "Way more fun, you say. This is easy, you say."

Jack laughed and hit the sack to her.

She missed, picked up the sack, and tossed it

to him. "I've changed my mind and think we'd be better off playing dodgeball."

He laughed. "You seemed interested until you found out they were playing with water balloons."

"Getting hit by a water balloon is appealing more and more," she mused as she missed the sack again. "In this heat, being doused with water would be a good thing, right?"

His grin was lethal. "That's what I was thinking."

His tone was both suggestive and teasing. Unable to repress her smile, Taylor shook her head and tried again to hack the sack.

"You'll catch on. Here, let me show you." Jack put his hands on her hips, then guided her leg through a series of motions where the bag rested on the medial aspect of her foot.

"Now, let's try an inside foot delay. Just catch the sack. Don't worry about doing anything with it at this point." From about her chest height, he dropped the ball onto her foot.

It fell to the ground.

He walked her through the motions again. This time it rested on the inside of her foot. Over and over, he repeated his lesson until she was lifting her leg to catch the bag when he dropped it.

"You're doing great," he encouraged when she

went several times in a row without missing. "Now, let's try with the other foot."

His patience amazed her and slowly she began to try to mimic the motions he walked her through time and again.

Soon a few others joined them on the grassy open area. Several others also had foot bags. Who knew people actually did this?

Before long, someone had music going and a foot bag challenge was on.

"Yeah, I'm sitting this one out." Taylor tossed the sand-filled ball back to Jack. "You've got this."

Waggling his brows, he and a half-dozen others kicked sacks around. After a few minutes only Jack and a guy named Will were moving to the beat, keeping their sacks in the air. A crowd gathered around them, chanting and urging them on.

"Go, Jack! Go, Jack!" she cheered, along with several others.

Will had his own cheer section, too.

"They're making this look too easy," a guy complained. "Someone get them a drink. We're going to add a new element to the competition to speed things along."

Two drinks showed up within seconds and were handed to Will and Jack.

Jack finished off his drink, keeping his sack

in the air. Will did as well, but with kicks that sent the sack high into the air over his head, and he'd kick it back up from behind him, then repeat the motions, all while chugging his drink. His movements were so fluid he looked as if he'd done the trick a zillion times.

When he'd finished his drink, loud cheers went out.

Laughing, Jack caught his foot bag in mid-air and bowed. "You are the master."

The crowd clapped. Soon a group game started up of sacking it up.

"Come on," Jack encouraged, taking Taylor's hand. "You have to play, too."

Taylor wanted to say no. It's what the old Taylor would have done, claiming she just wanted to watch.

But she didn't want to just watch.

She wanted to do more than sit on the sidelines.

Even if she failed miserably.

She wanted to live. Not just exist but *live*.

The sack made it all the way around and Taylor managed to catch Jack's toss with the center of her foot and kick it to the person to her left without letting it touch the ground.

She was unable to hold in a big "Yes!" and do a little victory dance.

A giggly girl with flowers in her hair and an

itty-bitty bikini on her equally itty-bitty body missed her toss during the second round.

No one seemed to mind and they started back over at round one.

The few times Taylor recalled being involved in games, there had been such a competitive element she hadn't had fun. She wasn't even sure those games had been about having fun, just winning. That wasn't what this was about. The smiling, happy people around her just wanted to enjoy being alive and at the festival. Wow.

Taylor wasn't sure how long they played, but they did so until a midday comedy show drew several away. Taylor took a break to rehydrate and reapply sunscreen.

"Need help with your shoulders and the back of your neck?"

She started to tell him she had it, but only a fool would turn down Jack's offer. "Please."

Squirting a generous portion of lotion onto his palm, he then rubbed his hands together.

"I doubt that's needed today," she mused, appreciative, though he'd thought to warm the lotion prior to applying it. Jack was a thoughtful man. She liked that.

She liked him.

"You're probably right." He placed his hands on her exposed shoulders, running them slightly beneath the edge of her sleeveless T-shirt, then down her arms.

Goosebumps prickled her skin.

Um…yeah, she liked that, too.

Next he got her neck. "Turn."

Knowing it wasn't the heat that melted her insides, Taylor turned.

"Here." He carefully applied fresh sunscreen to her face, then smiled. "You're quite beautiful, Taylor."

Despite the lack of make-up and grooming, despite the damage the sunshine and heat from the games had likely done, the way Jack was looking at her made her feel beautiful.

"Thank you." Her smile was as real as they got, coming from the inside out. "You need me to do you?"

His eyes sparkled.

"Apply sunscreen, that is?" she clarified, her lips twitching as she fought to keep a straight face.

"I'm good."

She bet he was. She didn't mean his lack of need for fresh sunscreen either.

A game of Ultimate Frisbee started and the others called them back over.

Taylor had never played with a foot bag but, thanks to Amy, she had played Frisbee on occasion during college. She wouldn't be performing any tricks, but she could hold her own by making decent catches and throws. It was one of the few team sports she had any experience with as her parents hadn't pushed for her to play as a child and she'd been busy with work and school once she'd gotten older.

About twenty people divided up into two teams. Skin versus shirts. Taylor was a shirt. Jack was not.

Watching him pull off his T-shirt had the same effect as him unleashing a secret weapon. One that left her slack-jawed and entranced.

The man had a beautiful body.

Taylor and the flower girl seemed on the same wavelength when it came to throws and they often made plays to each other.

Of course, Jack chose to try to block her catches. Tried and succeeded more often than not. Taylor attempted to reciprocate, but his reach outdid hers so he easily made his catches.

When their teams were tied nine each, Taylor decided to take matters into her own hands when Jack's teammates went to toss him the Frisbee for the winning point.

She leapt on him, wrapping her arms and legs around him.

Surprised, Jack caught her rather than the Frisbee, which landed a few feet away and rolled.

"Woo-hoo, looks like Jack caught more than he bargained for," one of the guys called out.

Another let out a wolf whistle.

"Are we playing tackle Frisbee or what?" another ragged, grabbing hold of his girlfriend's waist and pulling her to him for a kiss. "I'm all for a game of that."

Jack hugged Taylor, then let her slide down his body to stand, still flush against him.

Flush against Jack was hot.

Not because of the sun beating down on them. Or even because he was shirtless—although his damp skin was hot in more ways than one.

What was hottest was what she saw in his eyes, the way she felt his body tighten and his breathing hike up in intensity.

"You know this means war, right?" he teased, low and with a bit of a growl to his voice.

"Oops. Was I not supposed to do that?" she asked with feigned innocence, drawing a laugh from several of their teammates.

"Hey, baby, you can do that to me anytime you want," one of Jack's teammates offered.

"See what you started?" Jack accused with a laugh. "Now they're going to rewrite the rules and we guys don't stand a chance."

"Game on." A cute girl with a painted face, cat ears, short blue denim cut-off shorts, and a bikini top, who was on Taylor's team, picked up the Frisbee and tossed it to another teammate.

"Here, I'm open," Taylor called.

"No, she's not," Jack corrected, bear-hugging her and lifting her off her feet.

But the guy who'd had the Frisbee had already tossed it and somehow, hiked up in the air in Jack's arms, Taylor managed to catch it, much to her amazement and the excitement of her teammates.

"We win!" She bounced around in Jack's arms, waving the Frisbee over her head. "We won!"

Jack tossed her back over his shoulder, bum in the air, and carried her over to his teammates. "What should we do with this one? Pretty sure she deserves punishment."

A few lewd suggestions went up.

"Put me down, Jack Morgan," Taylor demanded, laughing so hard she could barely talk, and lightly smacking his bottom.

"Be careful what you start, Taylor."

For that, she pinched his very nice bottom.

"Remember, you asked for this." He lifted her from his shoulders and put her on her feet.

His words echoed from her past and a surge of panic hit. Taylor braced, preparing to defend herself, if needed. Her heart beat hard and heavy and she fought wincing.

But all Jack did was lean in and pop a kiss on her lips.

A very sweet kiss that was much more a reward than punishment.

Taylor's muscles sagged with relief, relaxing from the tension that had overtaken her. She should have known, maybe she had, but old habits died hard.

Taylor was having fun. Jack could tell by the big smile on her face as they danced to the beat of his favorite band. The group hadn't started playing until almost midnight. The crowd was really big so they hadn't tried spreading the blanket tightly folded inside his backpack.

Just as well. He liked watching the gentle sway of her body.

He liked how she looked relaxed and was soaking up the music. There was no hesitancy in her eyes, just trust when she looked at him.

Except for that moment when they'd been playing Frisbee and her big brown eyes had filled with uncertainty and fear.

He'd instantly connected her tension to his thoughtless words.

Her ex had a lot to answer for.

Thank God that look had been fleeting in her gaze and she'd shaken it off as quickly as it had appeared. Jack wanted her trust.

Wanted to deserve it.

He also wanted her.

But no way could he act on that want without the other medical staff realizing. Not that any of them would care, but being seen leaving Taylor's tent or her leaving his would cheapen what was between them, make her no different from anyone else he'd ever met.

Taylor *was* different.

He'd known it the moment he'd noticed the photo at Amy's and been drawn to it. Amy had come over and commented about how much she missed her friend since she'd married, how she worried things weren't as great as Taylor pretended. Knowing she was married, Jack had immediately written off his interest, but he'd never forgotten the smiling woman in the photo.

Taylor was unlike anyone he'd ever known and the way he felt about her was completely foreign to him.

So he enjoyed the moment they were in and let it be enough. When the crowd jumped up and down in time to the music, he and Taylor jumped. When the crowd jammed, they jammed.

Through it all they laughed and smiled and laughed some more.

It was an amazing night.

An unforgettable night that he didn't want to end.

* * *

This was it. It was now or never.

Pausing outside her tent, Taylor swallowed the lump in her throat and turned toward the man who'd become so important in such a short amount of time.

"I don't want tonight to end," she whispered. "Not yet."

She wasn't sure what she expected, but something more than Jack standing still, staring at her, then closing his eyes.

"I want you, Jack."

His lashes lifted, revealing tormented blue eyes.

Uncertainty hit her.

"I…" She paused, not sure what to say. Not sure why he looked torn.

He rested his forehead against hers. "You have no idea how much it means to hear you say that."

She could hear in his whisper that what he said was true. Her words had affected him.

"But I'm not going in your tent with you."

Her heart pounded. Was she so terrible at seduction? Should she have started kissing him rather than telling him what she wanted? Should she have just held his hand, unzipped her tent, and led him inside?

"Not because I don't want to," he continued.

His voice was so low she could barely make out his words. "But because I want to so much."

Taylor wanted to flip on her phone's flashlight and put him in the spotlight so she could better see his face. "That doesn't make sense."

Yeah, her frustration was audible. Good. Let him know she wasn't happy about what he was saying.

"Perhaps not," he admitted, "but it's true all the same." Lifting his head from hers, he planted a kiss where his head had just rested. "Goodnight, Taylor. I'll see you in the morning."

Jaw a bit slack, she watched him go to his tent. Without looking back and giving her the wink she'd come to expect, he disappeared into his tent.

What?

He was just going to sleep now?

With no more explanation than that?

Forget shining her phone light in his face. She wanted to throw the device at him.

Part of her wanted to let herself into his tent and go for what she wanted.

Wasn't that what the past few days had been about? That he wanted to have sex with her?

If not tonight, then when? They'd work from four p.m. to four a.m. tomorrow night—technically, *that* night. Had he forgotten?

Or maybe as he'd gotten to know her he'd decided they were better as friends than lovers.

No. She'd seen how he'd looked at her. She'd felt how he'd touched her, how he'd kissed and held her.

Jack wanted her.

So why had he just gone into his tent *alone*? Was he trying to be noble? Save her from herself?

Her hands went to her hips and she glared at his tent.

What if she didn't want him to be noble? What if she didn't want to be saved? What if what she wanted was to have sex with a man just because she wanted to have sex? Because she wanted what his body offered? Because she felt physical excitement when she looked at him? What if she wanted to not overthink what was happening between them and just feel, just act, just do, and live in the moment?

She bit the inside of her bottom lip. She'd never been a seductress. Although Neil had initially thrilled at her lack of experience, he'd soon pointed out her shortcomings when it came to pleasing a man.

She should go into her tent and be done with this.

She should.

But she wasn't going to.

Because she wasn't the love-starved woman who'd married Neil. Neither was she the beaten-down woman who'd finally had enough and walked away from what she'd no longer been willing to bear.

She was a woman who was stronger, who was figuring out who Taylor was, what Taylor wanted out of life, and was determined to enjoy the journey to figuring those things out.

She didn't fool herself that Jack was anything more than a pleasant stop along that journey. One she'd look back on with fond memories and smiles and maybe even a few regrets.

Was she willing to let this moment pass and not take that next step? Not let him show her what she'd been missing out on for the first twenty-five years of her life? Because she knew sex with Jack would be nothing like anything she'd ever known.

A mosquito buzzed around her and she swatted it away.

Now or never, Taylor. Are you brave enough to go for what you want? Or live the rest of your life wondering what would have happened if you'd gone into his tent?

Have you shed enough of the insecurities of the past to march over to Jack's tent and do everything in your power to make memories rather than regrets?

CHAPTER SEVEN

IGNORING THE FACT Taylor hadn't budged from where he'd left her, Jack stripped off his T-shirt and shorts and lay down on top of his sleeping bag.

He closed his eyes, the surprised look on Taylor's face haunting him.

Haunted him because the surprise had been replaced with uncertainty and hurt.

He didn't want her to doubt herself, or that he wanted her.

But he'd had to step away while he still could.

He'd explain to her tomorrow why he'd had to make an abrupt exit.

The tent zipper gave way.

No.

Yes.

Jack's heart pounded so loudly everyone probably thought one of the bands had taken the stage again.

He propped himself on his elbows, staring across the dark tent at Taylor's silhouette, watched as she closed the tent flap, then, looking his way, stripped off her T-shirt and shorts.

Hell.

How he longed for light so he could permanently etch into his mind the memory of what she looked like at this moment.

Darkness was good. He needed to send her away.

"What are you doing, Taylor?"

She didn't speak, just climbed in beside him and snuggled next to him on his twin-sized air mattress.

Her bare body pressed against his, which was only covered by his underwear, drove the nail home.

He could tell himself he needed to send Taylor away, but it was too late for that part of his brain to take control again.

Pulling her as close as their bodies would allow, he cupped her bottom, keeping her firmly against him as he covered her lips with his.

Sweet heavens. She tasted good.

He caught her soft sigh of relief and then lost himself in the desperation of how she returned his just-as-desperate kisses.

He wanted to see her, to know what was showing in her eyes as he ran his hands over her breasts, her hips, between her legs. But to turn on any sort of light would illuminate them to anyone walking by so he used his other senses to immortalize her.

The feel of her. The taste of her. The smell of her.

When she was ready, he donned a condom, maneuvered to where he was positioned just right, thrilled at how her fingers dug into his shoulders as he pushed inside, fought losing control at her soft whimper of pleasure as he moved his hips and she wrapped her legs around him, taking him as deep as he'd go.

Fighting to hold in his desire to roar, Jack brought her to the brink over and over until she desperately clung to him, quivering with her release, until his own body refused to hold back another moment and he lost himself.

His breathing hard, his chest feeling as if it was going to burst open, he collapsed on top of her. Then, worrying he was too heavy, he went to roll off, but she stopped him.

"Don't," she whispered. "Let me enjoy this for a little longer before you roll over to go to sleep."

Was she kidding him?

No way was he rolling over to go to sleep when she was naked and in his bed. But her words reminded him of how fragile she really was, of why he shouldn't have allowed what had happened to happen in a tent where they'd had to keep quiet, had needed to limit their body movements, had had to restrain the guttural reactions to just how good the other felt.

Because he had no doubt Taylor had felt good.

His own body tightened again. She'd wanted him to stay where he was, so she had no one to blame except herself when he started nuzzling her neck and running his hands over her body. Again.

Because that's what he wanted.

To touch her all over.

This time slower, surer, making it all about her, catching her moans with his kisses.

Jack wasn't sure what time Taylor had left his tent, but he woke alone, naked, and feeling a lot better than a man should feel who'd only slept a few hours.

At least, he thought it had only been a few hours. Stretching his arms over his head, he acknowledged that for all he knew it could be afternoon.

His tent was hot enough for it to be midday.

He dressed, unzipped the tent, and stepped out, immediately looked toward Taylor's tent. She was nowhere to be seen.

"Haven't seen her since early this morning."

Raking his hand through his hair, Jack turned toward Duffy. The older man sat in a chair, a soda in one hand and his cellphone in the other.

"'Bout what time would that have been?'"

"You mean when I saw her sneaking out of your tent or when she left to go and shower?" Duffy stared at him with narrowed eyes. "Or later when she came back, put her stuff away, then took off almost immediately rather than talk with me?"

He met the older man's gaze and knew there was no point in denying any of the accusations in his friend's eyes. Instead of saying anything further, he opened his cooler and pulled out a drink, took a long swig, then went over to where Duffy was sitting.

"Take your pick."

Duffy's stare was uncompromising. "You going to hurt that girl?"

Of all the people to see Taylor leaving his tent, why had it had to be Duffy? Jack leaned back in his chair. "Not planning to."

"You like her."

"Yes, and you're right. I'll probably hurt her," he acknowledged. He was the first lover Taylor had had since her divorce and that made her even more vulnerable, made him want to protect her all the more, even when that meant protecting her from himself. "Then again, she may end up hurting me."

Duffy laughed. "Yeah, right."

Jack shrugged. "Crazier things have happened."

Duffy's brow lifted. "Never known you to get caught up enough with someone to be hurt. Not since Courtney."

Yeah, Jack wasn't digging this conversation. Not for a thousand reasons. Duffy knew him well. As well as anyone really. Hadn't Duffy played a major role in influencing Jack's decision to straighten his life out? To become a doctor?

"We agreed not to talk about Courtney years ago."

Scowling, the older man shook his head. "Can't say I recall ever agreeing to that."

"Perhaps it was an unspoken agreement, but I thought you understood."

"I understand a lot of things. Like that you never let anyone get close enough to care about them and I'm worried about whatever this is with Taylor."

"There are a lot of people in my life I care about."

"Not what I meant, and you know it. Let's talk about Courtney and then you tell me why I saw Taylor coming out of your tent."

Jack glared at his long-time friend. "Have you been drinking something besides soda this morning or just feeling philosophical about your own life choices and trying to project them onto me?"

Duffy's expression hardened, but rather than respond he just stared at Jack with cynical eyes.

Hell.

Jack stood from the chair, crushed his empty drink bottle. "I'm done with this conversation and don't understand why we're having it anyway."

"Because of what I saw this morning."

"Because you saw Taylor leave my tent? It wasn't a big deal." Jack rolled his eyes. "You've seen women leave my tent before, seen me leave women's tents before," he reminded Duffy, "and you'll likely see it happen again in the future. Not once have you felt the need to comment. Not once. Do us both a favor and don't start now because Taylor leaving my tent meant nothing."

Taylor hadn't meant to eavesdrop on Jack and Duffy's conversation, but hadn't been able to avoid doing so. Not with their close proximity and the absolute agitation rolling off Jack.

She'd not known quite what to expect when they first saw each other this morning, but this upset, almost angry-sounding man wasn't it.

She'd not been able to sleep and after she'd heard the four a.m. crew leaving the campground, she'd snuck out of his tent in the hope of being inside her tent before the returning night crew showed.

Except for Duffy, who must never sleep, she'd succeeded.

Not that she'd seen Duffy but, from what she'd just overheard, he'd seen her.

That's when it hit her that she really didn't care that he'd seen her. As Jack had once told her, she was a grown woman and could do as she pleased. She'd pleased herself quite well the night before. More than once.

She wasn't ashamed of that. Actually, she was quite proud she'd gone to Jack's tent and climbed into his bed with him. To have done so had been so unlike the woman she'd once been and she liked that change. Liked it that she'd taken the initiative to go for what she wanted.

She had no unrealistic expectations. Jack was right. Her leaving his tent had meant nothing.

She wouldn't pretend that it had or that she'd wanted it to.

Daring Duffy or anyone to tell her she'd been wrong, she lifted her chin and made her way toward them.

Duffy's gaze went beyond Jack to meet with hers.

Jack spun, spotted her and cringed. "You heard that, didn't you?" He shook his head with disgust, looking very unlike the laidback man she knew. "Why am I asking? Of course you heard that."

That her smiling, happy Jack was anything but threw Taylor. She took a deep breath, pasted a smile on her face and went toward where the men were.

"Heard what?" She walked right over to Jack, planted a kiss on his cheek as if it was the most natural thing in the world to do and her heart wasn't pounding out of her chest. She held up the bags in her hands. "You won't believe the cool things I bought this morning."

Duffy knew she'd been standing there, had heard, but the older man didn't call her bluff. Neither did he comment on the fact she'd kissed Jack's cheek.

Why had she?

Because she'd needed to touch him? To remind herself that he was real? Or had that kiss been an attempt to calm him?

Then it hit her.

She was behaving as she would have with Neil.

No matter what had been going on, she'd pretend everything was fine to keep the peace, not make a scene, defuse his anger.

Startled at the realization, she lifted her gaze to Jack's.

Happiness didn't fill her. Neither did trust or a sense of safety.

Anger. That was what filied her.

Anger that he'd immediately revealed this new side and she'd immediately fallen into old habits.

She dropped her bags at her feet. "Actually, I did hear your conversation, but I don't understand why you're upset that I heard. Like you said, it meant nothing. Not to either one of us." Okay, maybe that had been exaggerating the truth a bit, but it had sounded good. "At no point have I had any expectations that you wouldn't be sneaking into women's tents in the future, neither have I had any desire for you not to," she added for good measure. "So what does it matter that I heard things I already knew and had no problem with?"

Jack's jaw tightened.

Although he didn't come right out and do so, Taylor would swear Duffy gave her a mental thumbs-up for her change in attitude. Jack, however, didn't look so thrilled.

"We need to talk."

She rolled her eyes. "Isn't that what we're doing?"

"Not here. Not where everyone can hear."

She glanced around the mostly deserted campground. "I don't think anyone is paying us the slightest attention."

"I am." Duffy spoke up, raising his drink to her. "I'm enjoying the entertainment."

"You would," Jack accused, throwing the man a *butt out* look.

"You just say that because you know I'm right," the weather-beaten man accused.

"Right? About what?"

Duffy's gaze flickered toward Taylor.

Rather than answer, Jack raked his fingers through his loose hair, then sighed. "Yeah, I guess you are."

Taylor didn't stick around, instead walked over to her car and put her purchases inside with a loss of the sunshine she'd felt when she'd bought the colorful sundress and scarf.

What Jack had said didn't matter. It didn't change anything. She'd already known she was just a fling. That was fine. That's all he was, too.

What mattered was how upset he was with Duffy. How abrupt.

No one always smiled so it shouldn't bother her that Jack was irate.

But it did.

Because old feelings had pitted in her stomach and ruined everything.

"I'm sorry."

At Jack's interruption, Taylor didn't glance up from the book she was reading. Not long after she'd dropped her purchases off in her car, she'd grabbed her bag, a book, and had taken off until she'd found a semi-shady spot to while away the afternoon until it was time to report for her shift.

"For?"

"You know what for."

"It's not a big deal."

"Tossing my words back at me?" He squatted down next to where she sat on a blanket on the far side of the event area. "I guess I deserve that."

"You're giving me more credit than I deserve." She hadn't even realized that's what she'd done until he'd pointed it out.

"I'm not giving you nearly the credit you deserve," he countered. "Last night was amazing."

Trying not to let his words get to her, she nodded. "This morning not so much."

"I am sorry you heard that."

She shrugged. "Don't be. We both know it's true." She took a deep breath, then continued. "And we are both okay that it's true. I'm just another festival fling for you and you're my post-divorce late rebound fling. We both got what we wanted and, like you said, it meant nothing."

He sighed, then gestured to her blanket. "Can I sit with you?"

Surprised that he'd asked, she nodded. "It's

not as if you aren't going to see me in a few hours during our shift."

"I needed to talk to you before then. To tell you I'm sorry."

Her hands shook. She didn't want him to notice so she set her book on the blanket, wrapped her arms around her legs, and clasped her hands together. "I don't understand your need to apologize, because you just stated what we both already knew. But, fine, apology accepted."

He let out a long sigh. "I've ruined everything, haven't I?"

She didn't understand. "What is there to ruin, Jack? Last night was amazing. We work tonight and leave in the morning. End of story."

"I don't want us to end this way."

I don't want us to end at all.

Her eyes widened in surprise at her unexpected thought. She'd known from the beginning they would end, that whatever happened was temporary.

She swallowed to moisten her dry throat.

"I've had a great time with you, Taylor. The best."

She could feel her eyes starting to water and didn't want to cry, didn't even know why she was on the verge of doing so, just knew she did not want to let him see her cry. "Please, don't do this."

His brows formed a V.

"Don't say things you don't mean." Had her voice sounded a bit desperate? She'd been going for strong, independent, *I don't care*, not pleading. She straightened her shoulders, tilted her chin, and willed her persona to be nonchalant. "Don't pretend any of this was more than what it was."

Next to her on the blanket, his body tensed and his eyes darkened. "What exactly is it you think we had, Taylor?"

"A romantic interlude that rebuilt my confidence in myself as a woman, in my sexuality. You gave me my post-divorce rebound sex. It was great. I'm very appreciative."

His forehead creased. "Is that what last night was? You using me for sexual empowerment? That's why you came in my tent?"

It wasn't. Not really. But maybe it was better if he thought it had been since he seemed to take his knight in shining armor role a bit too seriously. She didn't want him feeling responsible for her. She'd known exactly what she'd been doing and she'd had no expectations of him beyond that moment.

"Like I said, I'm good with what happened last night and with our saying goodbye tomorrow morning." She was, wasn't she? Of course she was. "Thank you."

His jaw worked back and forth once, then, without looking her way, he said, "No, thank you. Too bad I had to restrain myself so much or I could have made your reintroduction to sex more memorable. Still, glad to be of service."

On that note, he stood and walked away.

Taylor watched him go, wondering at the growing ache in her chest with every step he took, but patting herself on the back that she'd held herself together so Jack wouldn't have to feel guilty.

The medical tent was hopping when Taylor arrived. She'd gone early, signed in and gotten that day's T-shirt, and opted to walk there.

She'd needed the exercise to ease the soreness from her muscles and she'd needed the time to decompress before she started her shift with Jack.

Jack.

Sweet, wonderful Jack who felt responsible for what had happened the night before. She'd seen it in his eyes.

She'd given him an out and he'd taken it.

Because she'd been right.

All they'd ever been was a festival fling.

For that fling, she truly was thankful. Meeting Jack, being with Jack, having sex with Jack had healed so much of her lingering insecurities.

He'd made her feel desirable, worthy.

She was desirable, worthy.

She wasn't cold. She wasn't frigid. She wasn't immune to men. She wasn't dead inside.

She was passionate, hot, full of feminine fire.

She could enjoy her body, enjoy being a woman giving herself to a man.

Sex with Jack had unlocked a part of her that had been caged up during her marriage. Maybe it had always been caged up, waiting to be unleashed.

Regardless of the ache at how they'd ended, she would always be grateful to Jack for setting her passion free.

CHAPTER EIGHT

"So, DID THE two of you hit it off?" Amy questioned Taylor over the phone.

It was late Monday afternoon and Taylor had only been home long enough to shower, unpack and take a short nap that had been cut short by another phone call. One that had made Taylor's day.

"I asked Duffy how things were going a couple of times," Amy continued, "but he never would give me a straight answer and neither you nor Jack, when I texted with him earlier, told me anything."

Jack hadn't told Amy anything that had happened.

"What did Duffy say?" she asked, her mind still wondering at Jack's silence. They'd parted on good terms overall. He'd apologized a few dozen times about what she'd heard him tell Duffy and their goodbye had been a bit awkward. But Taylor had no regrets about their fling or their goodbye.

"I told you that he wouldn't give me details beyond that everyone liked you and you seemed to be enjoying yourself." Seeming to catch on, her friend redirected her questioning. "What *could* he have told me?" Amy asked with giddy emphasis.

Someday she would tell Amy all about her adventure with Jack. Today wasn't that day. For now, what had happened between her and Jack was private, special and outside the ordinary.

For Taylor, he'd cut away the last of the weights that had held her down. She was ready to embrace her future.

"What Duffy should have told you is that he, Jack and I worked the tent together and I think they are both wonderful men."

Very true. They were both wonderful men. Both modern-day gypsies of a sort. Both very special in their own ways.

"That's it?" Disappointment coated her friend's words.

Taylor could picture Amy's expression. Her forehead would be scrunched with doubt. Again, she was grateful Amy couldn't see her face as she might see more than Taylor wanted to reveal.

"If you're asking if your matchmaking paid off," she said, deciding to just address what Amy really wanted to know, "maybe Neil immunized me forever, especially from someone who's also a doctor. You know how I feel about that."

She felt guilty for deceiving her friend but when she and Amy were face to face she'd make sure Amy knew meeting Jack had been a good thing.

A great thing.

A spectacular and marvelous thing.

"Now, tell me about this guy you're seeing?" Taylor injected a lot of pep into her tone. "Jack mentioned you were dating his best friend. Give me details."

Amy's giddiness was almost palpable over the phone. "Dating might be presumptuous, but Greg is amazing. I want to be dating him."

"Jack seemed to think you two were an item already."

"Good to know," Amy admitted, sounding pleased. "But it's early days, especially as Greg doesn't live in Warrenville but about an hour away in Nashville. Long-distance relationships suck."

Yet another reason it was good she and Jack had ended when they had. Trying to keep up a relationship when they lived hundreds of miles from each other wouldn't have been any fun.

Not that they would have needed to have a long-distance relationship.

Taylor's stomach did an excited flip-flop.

Not for however long Jack would be working at the Warrenville emergency department.

"Speaking of long-distance relationships, I miss you," Amy told her. "How did your interview go?"

As thrilled as she was about the job in Warrenville, she was also a little nervous.

Because of Jack.

What they'd shared had been perfect, right? A beautiful interlude that had ended a little prematurely but which had otherwise been something from a fantasy.

Coming face to face with him day after day in the real world would dissipate their surreal experience. Then again, how much longer would he even be there before moving on to some other music festival or event?

"Really well." She'd barely hung up from the call when Amy's call had come in. "They offered me a position in the emergency room."

"What? Why didn't you tell me that first thing?"

"How could I? All you've talked about since we got on the phone is Jack." Ugh. Her tone had been a bit harsher than she'd meant it to. She wasn't anti-Jack by any means, but she did have reservations about being near him day after day.

"Sorry. I know I've gone on and on about

Jack." Amy sighed. "I really thought the two of you would hit it off."

They'd hit it off all right. Like electric sparks that sizzled.

"Obviously I've talked about him to the point of ad nauseam. Sorry," Amy apologized. "Forget Jack. I can't wait until you get here! I'll get the spare room cleaned out."

Taylor was just as excited and wished she could pack her things and leave for Warrenville this very moment. Instead, she'd work out her notice first.

"It's time you moved away from that town and memories of Neil," Amy continued in a more serious tone. "He's not worth holding onto, Taylor. Surely you've figured that out by now."

"Memories of Neil could never hold me here." If anything, they'd drive her away. "And I'm certainly not holding onto him. I fought hard to rid my life of him and can't imagine circumstances where I'd ever let him or any man steal my joy."

"You go, girl!" Amy praised. "Thank goodness you finally saw the light."

Taylor nodded. She had, right? That's why she'd let Jack walk away, let him think he hadn't mattered, right? Not that he'd offered, but she'd not wanted more. Not really.

Sure, had she met Jack years ago, before Neil, it would have been fun to have spent more time with him. The sex had been phenomenal. But she'd not been thinking long-term relationship. Neither had he.

"We'll have so much fun." Amy's excitement was almost palpable. "You moving here will be like old times. Plus, you'll be able to get to know Jack better."

"Amy, please don't push us together." Taylor took a deep breath. "Jack is a good guy. Thanks to you insisting that he babysit me, we watched a few concerts together, but it wasn't a big deal."

Liar, liar, pants on fire. Everything about Jack was a big deal.

Especially the sex.

Her pulse sped up just recalling how it had felt when she'd crawled onto his air mattress with him.

Taylor pushed back the memories. Rebound sex. Nothing more. Just rebound sex.

Very good rebound sex.

"And?"

"And nothing," she assured her friend. "Amy, we didn't even get to know each other well enough to exchange cellphone numbers. You're making something out of nothing."

True, yet not true. They hadn't exchanged numbers and yet she felt she knew him very well.

But the reality was that she didn't know Jack at all.

Taking the job in Warrenville meant having to come face to face with him again, but only for a short while.

Regardless, she'd never let another man prevent her from making the right choices for her. Taking the job in Warrenville and sharing an apartment with Amy was the right choice.

If Jack didn't like it that she'd be around, tough.

He could go work a music festival or something.

"Taylor starts orientation today. Isn't that great?"

Jack fought looking up from the chart he was finishing.

Thrilled her friend was relocating to Warrenville, Amy had talked about little else for the past month. Jack had been a bit blown away that Taylor would be in town, that he'd see her again, would get the chance to make up for his verbal blunder.

"Great," he agreed, and meant it. He was happy for Amy that her best friend was going to be close.

As for having his last two months in Warrenville interrupted by a beautiful blonde who'd turned his Rockin' Tyme experience upside down, well, worse things could happen.

Taylor was a beautiful, sexy woman with

whom he'd had a great time. Other than her having overhead his conversation with Duffy and the fact they'd had sex at all, Jack had no regrets.

Duffy had been right that Taylor deserved better than a music festival affair, and Jack wasn't a man who could give that to her. Still, he believed the affair had been good for her.

He knew the sex had been. For him, too.

Best sex of his life.

Why hadn't Taylor told her best friend they'd gotten together at the music festival? Was she ashamed that she'd had sex with him?

If anything, she should be ashamed of what he'd said to Duffy. He was. He hadn't gone into Taylor's tent because he'd wanted to protect her. Instead, he'd cheapened what they'd shared with defensive words spat out at the man who knew more about him than any other person.

Taylor was in Warrenville. As she'd done from the beginning, she'd fascinated him. But Duffy had been right to question him.

Sure, mentioning Courtney's name had thrown his hackles up, just as Duffy had known it would.

Jack had enjoyed a lot of relationships over the years, but no one had interested him the way Taylor did.

No one had even come close. Not since Courtney.

Wild, fun-loving Courtney who'd been his soul mate at the tender age of seventeen.

She'd been his first.

He'd been her last.

His eyes blurred and he blinked to clear them.

He was a rambling man, would only be in Warrenville for two more months.

Taylor had been hurt in the past.

Whatever he did, he had to be certain not to add to that hurt. He'd watched her confidence grow throughout the week, knew it was telling that she'd come to his tent, and could kick himself for his words, meant only for Duffy's ears, as he'd watched her deflate.

He'd also been proud when she'd lifted her chin and put him in his place.

Glancing up from the desk where he sat, he realized Amy had still been talking. He hadn't a clue what she'd said, or had asked apparently as she seemed to be waiting for an answer.

"Jack, have you heard a word I've said?" Amy demanded, hands on hips and giving him an expression she usually reserved for uncooperative patients.

Fortunately, he was saved from answering by a new arrival. Not that Amy didn't give him a knowing look before she took off to triage the patient.

A knowing look with a big smile.

A look she'd given him multiple times since Rockin' Tyme.

Taylor made her way down the Warrenville Hospital hallway to start her new employee orientation early on Monday morning.

A month had passed since she'd worked Rockin' Tyme.

A month in which she'd ended her apartment lease, packed her belongings, given what she wasn't taking with her to charity, and moved to Tennessee.

No. Big. Deal.

She had this.

The move had been accomplished over the weekend and she'd semi-settled into Amy's apartment.

Now she had a week of orientation prior to starting work in the emergency department. Even then, she'd be partnered with another nurse for the first few weeks for training on the electronic medical record system and hospital protocol. Then she would be on her own.

She'd worked the intensive care unit since graduation, but had enjoyed her emergency room rotation while in nursing school. She wasn't worried about her nursing skills. She was a good nurse and would take good care of her patients.

Her only hesitation about the entire move was seeing Jack.

How would he take her being in Warrenville?

Would he even care? How much longer would he even be there? A few months at most.

A few months that would fly by.

Regardless, her butterflies at seeing him had been unfounded as she made it through her first day without bumping into him once.

As she lay in bed that night, she wasn't sure if she felt relieved or disappointed.

Disappointed. a voice inside her head whispered. Definitely disappointed.

CHAPTER NINE

To HAVE NOT seen Jack the day before, Taylor started Tuesday morning out by almost crashing into him first thing in the hospital hallway.

"Jack," she rushed out, hating how breathless she sounded as she stared up into eyes so blue they pierced her. Just as quickly, she averted her gaze.

How could she have forgotten how intensely blue his eyes were? How masculine he was and how every female bit of her responded to that virility?

Face it, Taylor. Your body recognized what a potent man he was from the moment you laid eyes on him and went from zero to a hundred. He woke you up inside.

"Sorry, I wasn't paying attention to where I was going," she told him, staring at where his almost neon-green scrubs brushed over the tops of his equally bright tennis shoes.

"Taylor."

Her name on his lips dried up all the moisture in her mouth, making her tongue stick to her palate. She couldn't look at him and not remember, not ache inside at how it had felt to be beneath him, over him.

He'd made her feel really good.

Get a grip, Taylor. It was just a fling. Rebound sex.

"I heard you were starting at the hospital," he continued, causing her eyes to drift upward.

His smile was full and dug indentations into his cheeks. No doubt if she looked into his eyes they'd be all sparkly and happy.

Part of her felt all sparkly and happy at seeing him, too.

"From Amy, no doubt." Not having been prepared to see him so early after not seeing him at all the previous day, before even making it to her Tuesday orientation class, she stumbled over her words. "For the record, I interviewed for this job prior to arriving at Rockin' Tyme, before you and I had met, and I was lucky enough to land the job." Acclimating to the fact that he stood a foot away, Taylor steeled herself and met his gaze. "My being here has nothing to do with you or what happened."

His smile didn't waver. "I understand."

Did he? She hoped so. Only she hoped he didn't understand too much.

Like how good it felt to see him and yet how

part of her wished their paths had never crossed again so she could keep the memory of their night tucked away as something precious that had helped her along her path to discovering who Taylor was.

Trying not to stare, she reminded herself that she should get to orientation before they started without her or she lost her new job.

"That's good because, although it's good to see you—" definitely not a lie "—I don't want you to think I'm here because of you. I'm not." She gave a little laugh. She was rambling but wanted to make it clear that he shouldn't feel any type of obligation to her because of what had happened at Rockin' Tyme. "Honestly, considering, it would be simpler had we never seen each other again."

She pasted a cheery smile on her face. "But no worries. You'll be gone soon, right?"

Jack stared at the woman who'd haunted him for the past month.

Longer than that.

She'd haunted him since he'd first seen that photo in Amy's apartment.

Maybe a premonition of things to come?

He'd missed her.

Crazy.

They'd spent less than a week in each other's company and he'd missed her.

Taylor was here and for the next two months, they'd be working together.

Taylor kept her expression guarded. Despite the tension when they'd said their goodbyes, he hadn't thought she'd regretted what had happened, but regret was written all over her lovely face.

Of course she had regrets. Just as she'd likely been dreading their reunion. He'd been her rebound sex. Who wanted to come face-to-face with their rebound sex every time they went to work?

Lucky for her. Jack never stuck around any place too long and had already been in Warrenville much longer than anywhere he'd been since med school graduation. Soon enough he'd be out of here until next year's Rockin' Tyme.

The thought of leaving, of heading to the event in Daytona, should have his feet itching to get on the move. He loved his life.

Only he didn't like it that Taylor so obviously wanted him to hurry up and leave. Yeah, he didn't like that at all.

"Great to see you again, too." He gave a low laugh that echoed hollowly through him.

"Oh, I didn't mean…" Pausing, she winced,

then gave a repentant little shrug. "Um…can we just start over? Hi, Jack."

She glanced up, met his gaze for the briefest moment before her big brown eyes filled with panic and she shook her head. "I've orientation this morning. Probably wouldn't look good for me to be late my second day to work. Nice seeing you, Jack."

Before he could get out another word she took off down the hallway at a pace meant to get her away from him as quickly as possible.

Watching her go, Jack scratched his head.

Seeing Taylor again hadn't gone anywhere close to any of the dozens of different scenarios he'd imagined over the past month.

"Hope you don't mind, but I invited company for dinner."

Even before Amy finished her sentence, Taylor guessed who she meant and wanted to throw her cellphone across the room.

No. No. No.

She needed to tell Amy everything and just be done with it so her friend would let up.

"I knew you had bought stuff last night to make something yummy for dinner," Amy reminded her, "so, I invited Jack over. I told him what a great cook you are."

Gripping her phone tighter, Taylor winced.

Oh, Amy, what are you doing?

"My cooking skills are mediocre at best. Call and tell him you've changed your mind about the invite before I poison the poor man."

"But I haven't changed my mind," Amy insisted. "I'm almost home. Or maybe I should say we're almost home because he's following me. I just wanted to give you a heads-up so you could look your best."

"You know I was looking forward to a night with just you and me catching up, right?" Taylor sighed. "I think I'm going to put on my oldest, most ragged outfit and toss flour everywhere."

"We'll have plenty of time to catch up." Amy had the audacity to laugh. "And just remember, you make the mess, you have to clean it up."

In spite of having her evening plans completely changed, Taylor's lips twitched with a smile. "I thought it was if one cooks, the other one cleans."

"Is that how we used to do things?" Amy sounded amused. "Get to tossing that flour, then, cause we're almost there and if I'm busy cleaning the kitchen, that leaves you alone with Jack, right?"

Taylor sighed. How was she going to convince her friend to quit with the matchmaking?

Why was Jack going along with her anyway? Or did he realize that's what Amy was doing? Maybe he thought she just wanted to talk about Greg?

Maybe that did push Amy to keep trying. After all, wouldn't it be cool for two best friends to be dating two best friends?

But it wasn't going to happen. Not for her and Jack.

Taylor was making a new life for herself and that new life didn't include a relationship.

Especially not one with a man who was a doctor who she already knew wouldn't be sticking around long.

"This is really good," Jack praised, not surprised that Taylor was a good cook, and not because of Amy's glowing reviews. Long before that he had been sure Taylor could do anything she set her mind to do.

"Thank you."

Looking back and forth between them, Amy gave a big grin and asked, "So, Jack, who was your favorite act at Rockin' Tyme this year?"

Jack named the band that had been playing when Taylor had kissed him.

Although she'd been smiling and participating in the conversation, Taylor stared at her dinner plate as if she thought it might engulf the rest of her food.

"Although…" he named a band they'd danced and partied to "…gave a really good show, too."

Amy had grilled him multiple times at the ER about the festival, so her questions had to all stem around the fact that Taylor sat across from him.

If he moved his leg, no doubt it would brush up against hers.

He didn't move. It wasn't his place to purposely touch her if she didn't welcome his touch. But hell if he was just going to be complacent that she hadn't forgiven him for his stupid, careless words to Duffy.

"I'm still sad I missed it," Amy whined, her gaze going back and forth between Jack and Taylor.

"There's always next year. What about you, Taylor?" he asked, determined to pull her into the conversation. "You signing on for Rockin' Tyme next summer?"

Eyes wide, she shook her head. "Doubtful. I'll be busy."

Amy frowned. "Doing what?"

Taylor shrugged. "One never knows what life is going to throw at her. I mean, you had planned to go this year and that didn't happen."

"But you plan to sign up, right?"

Deciding to rescue Taylor from Amy's probing, Jack asked, "How is your grandmother, Amy? Still recovering nicely from her fall?"

Amy nodded. "According to my mother, yes. According to Granny, no. I'm planning to see for myself weekend after next."

Seeming surprised, Taylor's gaze lifted. "You're going out of town the weekend after this one?"

"Sorry. I just decided for definite earlier today. No worries. Jack will give you a good intro to Warrenville and keep you company. Won't you, Jack?"

Jack wanted to show Taylor Warrenville, but he didn't want to force his presence on her.

Like tonight.

He shouldn't have accepted Amy's invite. So why hadn't he said no?

Because he'd wanted to see Taylor.

It was for the same reason he said, "I'd love to if Taylor's not busy and wants to go."

"You did this, didn't you?"

Taylor watched as Jack ran his finger along the fluid lines of the sculpture. Although she loved the piece she'd given to Amy, causing her friend to gush on and on about how good it was, Taylor still felt insecure about her art.

"You don't have to answer," Jack assured her,

still eyeing the piece. "I know you did. She's beautiful."

Her breath caught. "She?"

"It's a woman," he explained needlessly. "A woman dancing on the water."

Taylor doubted most people could look at the foot and a half piece and immediately see the sum of the lines and curves.

Stunned by his insight, she admitted, "I'm impressed you see that."

Glancing her way, he added, "It's you."

Her throat threatened to close. Jack saw too much. "I made the piece, yes."

His expression softened. "Not what I asked."

He knew. He looked at the piece and he knew, had seen the truth. Why did that make her feel both vulnerable and ecstatic?

Staring into his eyes, she confessed, "Some days I think she's me. Others, she's who I want to be, free and not afraid of anything, not even walking on water." With a half-smile on her face, she shrugged. "My reality is most likely somewhere between drowning and treading water."

As if he understood what she meant, he nodded again. "I'd like to see more of your work."

"Why?"

He gave her an odd look. "Because you're good and I'm interested in seeing what you've created."

"I've only done a few pieces." That she'd show anyone, at any rate. She hoped to get started again soon. Finding a local art studio where she could work was still on her list of things to do. "For the record, I don't think of it as creating something, more an unleashing of what's locked away inside the clay."

Jack studied her, making her feel exposed, like he could see deep inside her to her thoughts. Then again, hadn't she thought the same when they'd been at Rockin' Tyme? The man saw past her shell to what she had hidden inside.

"You're very talented," he finally said, and sounded sincere.

"See, Tay," Amy announced, coming back into the room from taking a bathroom break. "I'm not the only one who thinks you're amazing."

Eyes locked with Taylor's, Jack grinned. "Definitely not the only one. She is very talented."

Taylor's cheeks heated. Why did she get the impression he wasn't talking about art anymore?

Why did that excite her?

Because Neil had made her think she was abnormal and dull? Because, for all her therapy and growth, a part of her had believed him until she'd met the man running his finger lovingly over her sculpture?

She wasn't abnormal or dull. She was passionate and creative and still unpeeling so many buried layers of who she was, of who she wanted to be.

Just like with the clay, she was unleashing the real Taylor.

"Thank you, Jack." She didn't mean for his compliment regarding her sculpture either.

Eyes sparkling, his smile wrapped around her and threatened to pull her close. "You're welcome, Taylor."

Taylor fought gulping, turned away from him, but made the mistake of looking Amy's way.

Her friend was grinning from ear to ear. Ugh.

She really needed to be more careful or Amy was going to think she was onto something with her matchmaking.

Maybe if circumstances were different, she might give in to the temptation she saw in Jack's eyes. She was in Warrenville to start fresh, not rekindle something that would be over almost as quickly as it started. She wasn't having a man and possible heartbreak interrupt the normal, happy life she was carving for herself.

Taylor didn't bump into Jack the following day at the hospital. Which gave her an emotional reprieve as she knew it was the last day of his three on, four off shift.

Unfortunately, Amy refused to let her enjoy that reprieve.

"A bunch of friends is getting together for dinner and drinks. I want you to meet them. Get ready and go with me."

Glancing up from where she was reading an article on antibiotic resistance, Taylor reminded Amy, "You don't have to invite me to go with you everywhere you go."

She didn't want to be antisocial, but she'd never operated on Amy's high level of social activity. Her friend had always been able to go, go, go.

"I know that and I don't." Amy's hands went to her hips. "You didn't hear me inviting you to go with me to my grandmother's, did you?"

Taylor rolled her eyes. "What I heard was you trying to throw Jack and me together, because he will be there, won't he?"

"Jack is my friend. Of course he'll be there." Amy gave a little so-what shrug. "Besides, you like him. I see it in your eyes when you look at him."

"I wouldn't be looking at him if you'd quit throwing us together," Taylor reminded her, putting her magazine down.

"Inviting you to go with me tonight has nothing to do with those looks I see passing back and forth between you and Jack."

Taylor eyed her friend suspiciously. "I don't

need to be babysat. A year ago maybe, but now I'm content spending time alone and just enjoying life."

She really itched to unpack her supplies, make a space in one corner of her room and get her hands wet with her clay.

Watching Jack touch her sculpture the night before had her fingers eager to mold and shape new pieces.

No, not pieces. One particular piece that was starting to take hold in her mind. She couldn't see it, just knew it was there, obscured from sight and necessary to be found by touch, necessary to be set free from the excess clay surrounding it.

"Yeah," Amy said, "except I don't see you enjoying life when you are sitting on the sofa, reading work-related articles."

"I've only been moved in a week," she said. "Should I have been throwing a party or out all night repeatedly during that time?"

"No, but you do need to quit hiding yourself away."

"Too bad I didn't hide myself away when I met Neil."

"Neil was an idiot, stuck on himself," Amy announced matter-of-factly.

Taylor snorted. "Agreed, and I married him. What does that say about my judgment?"

"That you should let me choose all future dates."

Taylor rolled her eyes. "You're under the assumption I want to date. I don't. I really am happy with where I am in life."

Mostly.

"Fine. You don't want to date and are happy with where you are in life. Now, about dinner, because you have to eat…"

She'd lived with Amy throughout college. Her friend wasn't going to let her sit at home alone. "By going to dinner with you and your friends, what you mean is going to dinner with you and Jack?"

"Not just Jack and me. There will be others, too." Not looking one bit guilty, Amy laughed. "I always did say you were the smart one in our friendship."

Knowing Amy wouldn't relent, Taylor stood from the sofa, stretched, and wondered if she should change. "That's not how I remember it."

"Yeah, well, your memory might be a little foggy. Good thing you're here for me to remind you of all the fun times we used to have."

Dinner with friends consisted of several co-workers meeting at a local bar. There were nine in total, so their waitress pushed two tables together and pulled a chair to one end.

Jack took the chair on the end.

Taylor went to move to the opposite end of the table but, as luck would have it, everyone else was already in the process of sitting down.

Grinning at her foiled efforts, Amy took the chair opposite where she stood, leaving only one unclaimed chair.

Right next to Jack.

"If I didn't know better I'd think you were trying to avoid sitting next to me."

She sank into the seat and gave him a pert smile. "Good thing you know better."

He stared at her a moment, then offered, "I will move my chair to the other end of the table if you want, Taylor."

Quit being so nice, she wanted to scream. Instead, she shook her head. "There's no need for that."

The waitress took drink orders. Everyone up to Taylor ordered beer.

"A water with lemon, please."

"Ah, Tay, loosen up and have some fun," Amy encouraged.

Taylor just smiled at her best friend and was grateful when the waitress took Jack's order then left to get their drinks.

"Afraid to lower your inhibitions around me?"

First making sure Amy was caught up in her

conversation with the phlebotomist sitting next to her, Taylor cut her eyes to Jack. "Should I be?"

"No." but the promises in his eyes warned otherwise. "Unless you're still upset with me about what I said to Duffy."

She shook her head.

"In which case, there's no reason why we can't be friends."

"Friends." Taylor let that sink in. Jack wanted to be her friend. "Is that what you want from me? Friendship?"

His gaze darkened. "Until a few days ago I thought I already had your friendship. Now I'm not sure."

"You did." Taylor sighed. "You do," she corrected, knowing it was true. How did she explain she'd enjoyed their tryst but didn't want to pick up where they'd left off? But that she feared her body wouldn't go along with that plan given half a chance?

The crinkles at the corners of his eyes fanned outward. "I'm glad. You have to admit we had a good time."

She couldn't deny it. Neither did she want to discuss their "good time" at a table of their co-workers, especially not as she could feel Amy's curious looks.

"Right. The concerts were great. I really appreciate you keeping me from going alone. Now, tell me about where you'll be headed for your next music festival."

Yes, she was changing the subject. To his credit, he let her.

"I don't have another until after my gig is up here in Warrenville. Then I'm off to Daytona for a country music weekend event."

"Country music?"

"Yep." He glanced around the bar where they were and stage-whispered, "In case you haven't noticed, we're knee deep in country in this place."

She had noticed the handful of couples out on the dance floor and the twangy music playing in the background.

"I didn't know you liked country."

"There's a lot you don't know about me." He grinned. "Yet."

"There's a lot I do know about you," she mimicked in a low voice. When she looked up, Amy had given up all pretense of conversation with the woman next to her and was watching them like a proud mother hen.

Straightening her napkin and ignoring Amy, Taylor asked, "So, which is your favorite? Country or rock?"

"I like and listen to both. Not sure I like one genre better than the other. Certain artists stand out more than others from both genres, but I really don't lean more one way than the other overall. What about you?"

"We've established that I'm not a big music buff."

"I thought we'd resolved that at Rockin' Tyme. You seemed to get into the swing of things." He grinned. "Literally."

She laughed. "Some random guy grabbing me and tossing me about a bit doesn't count as me getting into the swing of things."

Amy pounced. "I didn't hear about this random guy. Tell me more."

Taylor shrugged. "It wasn't a big deal. Jack and I were dancing and a fellow Rockin' Tymer wanted a turn."

"You danced?" Amy's eyes sparkled.

Feeling quite proud of herself, Taylor nodded. "I told you that I know how to have a good time. Why won't you believe me?"

Although she looked impressed, Amy shot back, "I keep waiting for you to show me."

"That's my cue if ever I've heard one." Jack pushed his chair back, stood, and put his hand out to Taylor. "Dance with me and show this skeptical lady what I already know."

Feeling pretty skeptical herself, Taylor arched a brow. "What's that?"

"That you know how to have a very good time."

CHAPTER TEN

TAYLOR STARED AT Jack's hand as if he were the Grim Reaper come to lead her down a dastardly path.

It wasn't a look Jack enjoyed seeing on her pretty face, but they needed to get away from the table and Amy's listening ears for a few. The dance floor offered that reprieve.

Rather than decline, she reluctantly put her hand in his, shot a glare toward Amy, who laughed, then let him guide her to the dance floor.

"You know the waitress is going to take orders while we're here, right?" she pointed out while following him to the far corner of the dance area. The other dancing couples didn't offer much shield from their co-workers' eyes, but at least their conversation couldn't be overheard.

"She'll come back," he said. "May I?"

"I think it's a given that you're going to since we're here to dance." She eyed him curiously.

"Do you think this is a good idea with everyone watching?"

He wrapped his arms around her, letting his hands rest at her waist. At first she stood awkwardly against him, then sighed and put her arms around his neck.

Holding her again felt so good, so right.

"Let them wonder."

"Easy for you to say," she mused. "You're leaving in a couple of months."

He pulled back enough to look into her eyes. "You care what they think?"

She considered his question, then shrugged. "Only Amy."

"She approves."

Taylor snickered. "You think?"

He did his best to look innocent. "I've picked up on a few hints here and there."

Taylor rolled her eyes. "Observant of you."

"What about you?"

She arched her brow.

"Do you approve?"

"Of our dancing?" She shrugged. "I'm here, aren't I?"

"That you are," he agreed, pulling her closer as they swayed to the music. "You feel good, by the way."

She smelled good, too. A light vanilla with a dash of spice scent drew him in, making him want to inhale deeply. Cookies, he thought. She reminded him of fresh-baked sugar cookies.

"And," he continued, "I've missed you."

Her gaze lifted, but it wasn't a smile on her face. No, she was frowning. "How could you have missed me? We spent less than five full days together."

"Five great days that ended too soon."

She didn't look convinced. "What exactly did you think was going to happen Monday morning at the end of our shift? That we'd make plans to drive to see one another until the sexual chemistry fizzled out? You didn't know about my interview or that I might move here before your ER stint was up so I know you weren't planning to see me again."

"You think our sexual chemistry would have fizzled out?" He ignored the rest of her comments, because he didn't know the answers.

She rolled her eyes. "Be serious, Jack."

"I was. It's been over a month and the chemistry is going strong."

She missed a step, bumping her foot against his. "It is?"

"Do you really have to ask?" Jack held her close, fighting the urge to lower his head to where he could breathe in the scent of her hair, of her neck, see if she tasted of cookies, too. "I don't like this tension between us." Such an understatement. "I can't figure out if it stems from my comment to Duffy or Amy pushing us together or something I'm clueless about. Regardless, I want you, Taylor. I have from the beginning and that's not changed. Not for me."

"If you wanted me so much, why did I have to come to your tent?" Her eyes glittered with challenge and her chin tilted forward. "Why didn't you come to mine?"

He deserved her questions and she deserved the truth. "I was trying to do the right thing."

She snorted. "Guess I blew that all to pieces."

"So that you know the whole truth, I was afraid you weren't ready to take that step and didn't want you to have regrets." He shrugged. "Unfortunately, you do anyway and that's my fault for my careless comment to Duffy."

"Why does any of this matter now?"

"Besides the fact that we're going to be working the emergency department together soon?"

"There is that," she admitted.

"But more importantly," he continued, "it matters because I wasn't ready for our relationship to end and I don't believe you wanted it to either."

"We ended one night early," she reminded.

Jack had never had difficulties talking to women. Now wasn't the time to start, but he was struggling to tell Taylor how he felt, what he wanted.

"I think you misunderstand." He searched for the right words. "I didn't want us to end on Monday morning, Taylor. That's why I didn't come to your tent. Because you meant more to me than just another woman I met at a music festival. I was doing my best to make sure you knew that. I thought if we had sex, I'd never convince you that I wanted a relationship."

"I wanted you to come to my tent."

"I needed to do things the right way."

"Whose right way, Jack? Yours? Mine? Someone else's? Because what makes you think your way was the right way? Or what I even wanted? I'm tired of men who think their way is the right way," she ranted, her brown eyes narrowed to tiny slits. "Who says I wanted a relationship? What if I just wanted sex and for us to go our separate ways on Monday?"

She had a point. Still, it wasn't as if he was asking for forever. Just that he enjoyed her company and wanted more of it. Wanted more of her.

Was he was being selfish in wanting to pursue a relationship when he'd be leaving?

Then again, she wasn't saying she wanted more.

"What is it you want, Taylor? Friendship?

Then we'll just be friends. If that's what you want, I'll respect your decision."

With all his heart he believed she wanted more than friendship. He felt it in her touch, in the way her fingers had found their way into the hair at his nape and toyed with it. "But, for the record, I want more than friendship."

Her feet were barely moving. "How much more?"

"I'm here for another two months."

"Beyond that?"

He inhaled. "Anything beyond that wouldn't be easy. Not with the way I travel." He exhaled slowly, not liking his next words. "Whatever happened would end when I leave Warrenville."

The song they danced to ended and another started. They continued to slow dance, but the tempo was more upbeat, matching the wheels turning in Taylor's head. He could see them spinning round and round, much as the other couples on the dance floor were.

"I miss you, too," she finally said. "But that doesn't mean anything is going to happen between us."

What she said registered and he laughed, pulling back and pretending to check her.

Taylor's hands stilled at his neck, where she'd been twisting his hair around her fingers. "What are you doing?"

"Checking for blood because I'm pretty sure that admission mortally wounded you."

She rolled her eyes, but the effect was lost as she was smiling. "Don't press your luck, Jack."

His arms already around her, his hands at her lower back, he hugged her. "In all seriousness, Taylor, I'm glad you miss me. I want you to miss me so much that, for the next two months, you can't stay away."

Her eyes took on a sparkle he'd not seen since Rockin' Tyme, other than when she'd been talking about her sculpting.

"Sounds a little creepy."

He laughed again. "There she is."

"Who?"

"The woman who captivated me during a music festival."

"Who do you think you had dinner with last night?"

"Someone who refused to let herself relax and enjoy being with me."

She closed her eyes. "Okay, I'll admit it. I don't want to want you, Jack."

"I know."

Her eyes opened. "Actually, the truth of the matter is wanting you at Rockin' Tyme thrilled me. It had been so long since I'd felt anything regarding the opposite sex. But now that I do feel, well, attracted…" she sighed, her warm breath caressing against the curve of his neck, "…it's inconvenient and doesn't fit with who I am or the life I want to make here. So, I want you but I don't like it."

There was so much sincerity, so much emotion in her voice it made his heart hurt for her. Made him want to protect her from ever adding to her leeriness or pain.

"We don't have to do this." Although convincing his body wouldn't be easy when she was melted against him so completely. "I was serious when I said we could be friends."

"I guess we'll see." She gestured beyond him. "The waitress has almost finished taking everyone's orders. We should join them."

Taylor wasn't sure who'd pulled what strings, but Amy was her orientation trainer. Amy had been an excellent nurse when they'd graduated. Her skills had only become more fine-tuned over the years since then and working with her was informative and enjoyable.

Working with Amy meant being on the same schedule as Jack.

Something Taylor was taking one day at a time.

Over a week had passed since their dance. A week in which she'd seen him more days than not, but always at work or in a social setting with others, sometimes just Amy.

Amy, who had bounced around with excitement and squeals of "I knew it!" when Taylor had confessed the truth about Rockin' Tyme.

Currently, Amy had gone to the lab to drop off a vial of blood she'd drawn as the phlebotomist had been tied up with another patient. She'd sent Taylor to assist Jack on a thirty-something man who had a laceration requiring closure.

Working with Jack was almost as awesome as working with Amy. He brought the same laid-back professionalism to the emergency room that she'd gotten used to at the music festival. He didn't get overly excited no matter what drama was unfolding, but was always on top of things medically. He treated everyone, staff and patients, with care and consideration.

He really was a great guy and a gifted physician.

"You want to finish closing this wound?"

Surprised at his question, Taylor glanced up to see if Jack was teasing.

He wasn't.

She'd only sutured a few times and none over the past few years as the opportunity hadn't arisen in the intensive care unit where she'd been working.

Did she want to? Not really. Especially not

with Jack watching. But she wasn't going to say no to a learning opportunity and Jack was a great teacher.

With trembling hands, she took the needle holder from him.

Following the pattern he'd made along the man's gashed arm, she positioned the needle, then looked at Jack.

"Perfect," he reassured her as she pushed the curved needle into the man's anesthetized skin and out the other side of his wound.

Pulling the thread through, she released the needle, wrapped the ethilon around the tip of her needle-nosed holder multiple times, then tied off a knot. She repeated the knot-tying process several times. She wrapped one direction one time and the opposite the next, to make sure the knot didn't work loose as the man returned to his normal activities of daily living and increased tension was placed on the sutures.

"Beautiful stitch," Jack praised.

Glancing up, Taylor smiled.

"It is, isn't it?" she teased, pleased with both his praise and the suture.

She put the next three stitches in, getting faster with the last one.

"Excellent. Don't you think so, Ralph?" Jack asked their patient, who'd been talking a mile a minute about his logging business and how this same thing had happened a few years back.

Ralph glanced down at his closed cut. "Looks good to me. This mean I can go home now?"

Jack laughed. "Soon. Taylor is going to dress your wound, give you a tetanus vaccination, and print out wound-care handouts for you. When she's done, I'll write discharge orders. Then you can go home."

Taylor finished cleaning the man's more minor cuts and scratches. Really, the guy had been lucky. He'd been cutting timber and, unexpectedly, a tree had fallen near him. Some of the branches had left nasty cuts. The one on his left arm had been the worst and the only one requiring sutures.

"Nice job in there," Jack commended when she returned to the nurses' station where he sat with Amy.

"Thanks." She gave him a smile she hoped conveyed her true appreciation of his patience and praise. "It's been a while since I've sutured so I was nervous."

"You did fantastically. You can assist any time on my patients, Nurse Hall."

"Thank you, Dr. Morgan." She met his gaze, wondering how any woman could ever resist the shimmering joy in his eyes. How she'd ever thought she could resist?

"Listen to you two being all normal co-workers," Amy teased, standing up from the nurses' station where she'd been charting. "There's another new patient in Triage. I'll attend to him."

Taylor watched her go and fought sighing.

"She's persistent. You have to give her that," Jack mused, not sounding upset by Amy purposely leaving them alone.

"And as subtle as a ton of bricks."

"Speaking of which, this is the weekend she's out of town. She made me promise to make sure you didn't sit home alone."

"We both know what happened the last time she made you promise to watch out for me."

He shrugged. "I liked what happened last time."

She had, too, but that didn't mean it should happen again. Getting all tangled up with a man was not on the agenda of her new life. It just wasn't.

She glanced down to read the information on the patient Amy was triaging. A four-year-old with shortness of breath with suspected asthma. She pointed it out to Jack and he left to take a quick peek at the boy.

When he returned, he dropped in an order for a nebulizer treatment. "Amy took a verbal and has already gotten the treatment started. She said to tell you she'd let you know if she needed you."

Next to him at the nurses' station, Taylor studied Jack as he documented his physical examination of the child.

"Do you like kids, Jack?" The question popped out of her mouth as quickly as the thought had hit her. Her throat dipped somewhere in the vicinity of the pit of her stomach.

Pausing at the computer, he turned toward her. His eyes sparkled as he said, "All except the whiny ones."

"They're all whiny at one point or another, aren't they?" Grateful he hadn't seemed to read anything into her question, she continued, "Honestly, I'm not one to give thoughts on kids. I was an only child and have little experience with children outside nursing school or work."

"Only child? That makes you spoiled rotten, right?" he teased.

"Ha. Hardly, Mr. Also-an-Only-Child." She shook her head. "My parents were in their forties when they got pregnant with me. They'd not planned to have kids, so I was a surprise they didn't want and didn't know what to do with once I arrived. I mostly did what they expected of me, stayed quiet and kept to myself as not to disturb them too much."

If she ever had children, she'd make sure they never felt that way.

"That doesn't sound like fun."

"Fun was not a word in the Hall household."

"Poor Taylor."

"Don't mock me," she scolded. "I didn't say I had a bad childhood, just not a fun one. My parents were strict. Not quite military-school strict, but I imagine they got close. They weren't mean or cruel. I was always taken care of. Never without food, clothes, shelter, books to read. I certainly didn't have it bad. Just not the stuff of Normal Rockwell."

He studied her a moment, then confessed, "I was home-schooled."

"Really?"

He nodded. "We traveled too much for me to attend regular school so my mother provided my education. It was interesting, to say the least."

Taylor lifted one shoulder. "You went to med school so she must have done something right."

"She did a lot right and got lucky that I liked to learn and was a good student."

"I wasn't."

"Wasn't what?" he asked.

"A good student," she admitted, a little embarrassed that she felt compelled to do so.

"I find that difficult to believe."

"Oh, don't misunderstand. I made good grades," she clarified. "I just had to work really hard for them. Amy could party all night, go to class the next morning and ace a test. Not me.

I had to put my nose to the books and learn the material inside out."

"Everyone learns differently."

"Yeah, some of us do things the hard way over and over." Glancing around the emergency room bay, which was rather quiet at the moment, restlessness overtook Taylor. "Guess I should see if Amy needs help."

"She's going to say she doesn't because she prefers you to be doing exactly what you are doing right this moment."

"What's that?"

"Talking with me."

Taylor sucked in a deep breath. "Jack."

He grinned. "I like it when you say my name."

"Yeah, well, I should say Dr. Morgan."

He shook his head. "No matter what happens, I'm always Jack to you. Always."

Amy left on Friday morning and Taylor's phone buzzed before ten a.m. with a text from Jack. She'd been up for a while, working on catching up on her laundry.

Staring at her phone, she sighed. *Oh, Jack. What am I going to do about you?*

She'd been clinging to what she'd overheard as an excuse to put distance between them. She recognized that just as she recognized the truth in what he'd said. She and Jack had no future together. Spending time with him set her up for heartache, but not spending time with him seemed impossible.

At least for as long as she was paired with Amy for orientation she'd be on the same work schedule as Jack. And, for at least as long as Amy had breath in her body, her friend seemed determined to push them together.

Jack's position at the hospital would be ending before long. Then she wouldn't see him. At all.

Just the thought of that made her heart squeeze.

Maybe she was only hurting herself by refusing him when she could be having sex with Jack. He missed her and wanted her. He'd told her so. Spending the next few weeks with Jack wouldn't derail her goals. She wouldn't depend on him or expect anything from him.

He was leaving. She knew he was leaving. She didn't want him to stay.

She'd be fine.

CHAPTER ELEVEN

TAYLOR'S HAIR WAS blowing about her face crazily as she and Jack rode in 'Jessica', his nickname for his Jeep. The sun beat down on top of her head. The radio was cranked up and could be heard over the wind noise.

Raising her arms above her head to let the wind blow through her fingers, Taylor laughed.

Jack glanced over at her and grinned. "Having fun?"

Between the air with the top off, the radio, and the engine, the Jeep wasn't conducive to having a conversation, so Taylor nodded her answer.

This was fun.

And a lot more relaxing than she'd have imagined.

They drove around on Tennessee back roads for more than an hour before Jack pulled over near a bridge.

"You want to walk down and play in the water?"

Taylor stared at him as if he'd lost his mind. "What?"

His eyes were full of challenge. "You heard me."

"I didn't bring clothes for playing in the water."

He waggled his brows. "Where's your sense of adventure?"

Good question.

"I was born with a genetic deficiency of that particular sense." But was working on developing it.

He laughed, grabbed his backpack from behind his seat, then climbed out of the Jeep. "Come on. If we hike just a short way, there's a cool waterfall. It's not big, only about six or seven feet, and flows down rather than being a straight drop, but it's a beauty with the way the water moves over the rocks."

"Do I even want to know how you know that?"

"I've been here before."

With a woman? she wondered.

Coming around to her side of the Jeep, he held out his hand. "One of the times Greg was in town, Amy, Greg, and I checked this place out. Amy is a treasure trove of off-the-beaten path places."

Taking his hand, she stepped out of Jessica. "Now I know why she's pushing us together."

"Why's that?" he asked, leading the way down the embankment to where the small river ran.

"So you'll quit being the third wheel on her dates with Greg."

He laughed. "You might be right."

Making it to the water's edge, Taylor took in the bubbling water with the big flat rocks scattered about. Small purple flowers grew along the banks, as did Queen Anne's Lace and Black-Eyed Susans. Beyond the bank was a field that led into woods. Everything in sight was absolutely gorgeous—the man included.

Tossing his backpack onto the grass, Jack kicked off his shoes and waded out into the water, which came just above his ankles.

"When will I get to meet Greg?" she asked as she sat down on the bank and began taking off her sandals. She had to at least dip her toes into the water. "I've been here a couple of weeks. They talk on the phone and text often enough, but I figured I'd have met him by now. He's only an hour away, right?"

"Amy would know better than me," Jack admitted. "But I imagine we've not seen him since you've moved in to give you two time to catch up. He'll probably drive up during Amy's next four days off. He was here almost weekly prior to your move."

She hadn't really thought about how her living at Amy's place impeded her friend's dating life. Amy had repeatedly invited her to move back in, but maybe her being there was an imposition?

"Good. I'm glad he's coming." Once she'd met him, she'd make herself scarce. "I need to make sure he's good enough for my best friend."

Holding his hand out to her as he waited for her to step into the water, he asked, "Turnabout is fair play?"

"Oh, Amy's not trying to make sure you are good enough for me. She gave her stamp of approval long before I'd ever met you." Taylor's eyes widened at how cold the water was. Her skin goose-bumped. "Wowzers, where are the ice cubes coming from?"

Jack chuckled. "This is fed from an underground spring about a mile from here and is a bit brisk when you first step in. You'll get used to it and it'll feel good in this heat."

The water temperature was definitely a direct contrast to the late morning sunshine, but Jack was right in that the longer she was in the water, the more she adjusted to the temperature.

A step ahead of her, Jack stopped walking, let go of her hand, and bent down to study the water in a semi-shallow spot where the creek bed was readily visible.

"Tell me you've not found a snake," she ordered, trying to see what he was looking at and not spotting anything. She took a step back, just in case.

"No, but it is possible we might see one. If we do, just don't panic. Odds are it'll be more scared of you than you are of him." At her look of alarm, he grinned. "No worries, Taylor. If anything tries to bother you, I'll rescue you."

"Yeah, yeah, but who's going to rescue me from you?"

He waggled his brows. "You have all the power where I'm concerned."

"What's that mean?"

"That whatever you say goes. That's why I haven't pushed this past week. Nothing will happen between us until you give the word that you're ready."

She was still pondering his comment when he reached down in the water and scooped up something with his hands.

Something that was alive.

"Don't throw that at me or I may never forgive you."

"I won't but come and see."

Taylor carefully made her way across the

rocky creek bottom to stare into Jack's cupped hands.

"Is that a baby lobster?"

Looking up at her, he grinned. "I take it you've never seen a crawdad before?"

She shook her head. "Is that what that is?"

He nodded. "Technically, it's called a crawfish, but you won't hear anyone around here call it that."

"Those are claws, though, right?"

He nodded.

"Will he pinch you?"

Jack shrugged. "It's possible but in all my years of catching crawdads I've yet to have it happen."

"You've done this a lot?"

"Played in creeks catching minnows and crawdads? My whole life."

"Music festivals and catching crawdads. Sounds a little idealistic, Jack."

One corner of his mouth lifted. "At times."

Sensing there was something more behind his half-smile, she asked, "And at others?"

He shrugged. "Nobody's life is perfect, but I have no complaints."

"Our childhoods couldn't have been more different."

"I take it your parents never took you to a creek to catch crawdads and minnows?"

She shook her head. "This is my first time in a creek and you already know I had no clue what a crawdad was."

He held his hands out toward her. "You want to hold him?"

"What?" She stared down at the less than two inches long mini-lobster in Jack's cupped palms. "I'm afraid to."

"If he pinches, I promise to kiss you and make you feel better."

Heart pounding, Taylor's gaze lifted to Jack's and suddenly holding the crawdad didn't seem nearly as scary as continuing to stare into his eyes. It would be so easy to fall for him. To become so head over heels that her experience with Neil would seem like child's play. To let how wonderful Jack was sway her life views to where she just didn't care that in the long run he'd hurt her if she wasn't careful.

"Don't let him hurt me," she ordered, then scrunched her forehead. *And don't you either.* "How do we do this?"

"Cup your hands like mine and scoop water into your hands."

She did as he said, then looked at him expectantly.

"I'm going to hold my hands over where yours are cupped and put him into your hands." His voice held the same patience she saw him exhibit in the emergency room. The same patience he seemed to exhibit in all aspects of life. "Ready?"

She nodded. She could do this. Not that she'd ever known she wanted to hold a crawdad, but in this moment overcoming her fear seemed paramount. Did that directly relate to her fear of letting a man close enough to hurt her? To change who she was or impede the discovery of who she was?

He put his hands directly on hers, his skin cool from having been in the water, then moved his hands apart slightly to let the water and crawfish he held drop into her hands.

"Oh, my," she said, nervous she held the creature, but excited she was doing so.

"He won't hurt you," Jack reminded her.

She didn't take her eyes off the crawdad. "You're sure?"

"Ninety-nine percent positive."

Her gaze lifted. His grin was lethal.

"That doesn't make me feel better, Jack."

He laughed. "We should have brought cups to catch with. Crawdads I can do bare-handed. It's been a while since I've caught a minnow that way, though."

"I didn't know we were going to be doing this."

"Gotta be prepared for anything when you're with me."

"You could have told me that before I said yes to coming with you," she teased, then deepened her voice to intone, "Taylor, be prepared for anything, because you may end up standing in the middle of a creek holding something that looks like a baby lobster."

His lips twitched. "Would your answer have been different?"

Eyes locked with his, she shook her head. "No, not as long as this thing really doesn't decide to pinch me and not let go. That happens and you're on your own."

"If he does, we'll make him lunch."

"Um...no." Taylor wrinkled her nose, then glanced down at the creature in her palms. "Do people really eat them?"

"Many consider crawfish a delicacy."

"Doesn't look like much of a meal."

"Yeah," he chuckled. "One wouldn't be."

"You eat them?"

He nodded. "On more than one occasion."

Her gaze dropped back to the tiny creature with empathy. "Let's let this one go."

"Guess it's a good thing I brought lunch, then."

"You brought lunch?"

He nodded and gestured toward his backpack. "Drinks are in the cooler in Jessica, though."

"You're like a scout. Always prepared."

He chuckled. "Never a scout, but I've camped more than my share."

She arched a brow at him.

"Most of my childhood was spent in campgrounds. There were a few times we lived in actual buildings, but they were far and few between."

"You lived in tents?"

"Sometimes. Most of the time we had this pop-up camper we pulled behind a mini-van my mother referred to as Bertha."

"That's where you get naming your Jeep?"

He gave her an incredulous look. "Have you never named a vehicle?"

She shook her head.

"Guess that's going to be another first for you, Taylor, because your car has to have a name."

"Yeah, well, my little sedan doesn't have Jessica's character. She'd be rather dull, I think."

"Your car is a female, then?"

She thought about it a minute, then nodded. "Definitely."

"Look, that one's a rabbit munching on a carrot." Taylor pointed to a group of puffy white clouds that contrasted starkly with the intense blue of the sky.

"I see the rabbit, but are you sure that's a carrot?"

She turned to look at Jack. "What else would it be?"

"A cigar. See the tiny puff of smoke coming off the end?"

"Okay, I'll give you that one." The clouds did look more like a rabbit smoking a cigar than one eating a carrot. "But, for the record, my rabbit was healthier than yours."

"You won't get any arguments from me on that one."

Something in his voice struck her and she turned her head to look at him in question.

Without looking her way, he admitted, "Both my parents smoked, which is why I lost my dad at too early an age."

"I'm sorry, Jack. What happened?"

"Heart attack in his late forties."

"You were young when it happened, then?"

"Fairly young," he agreed, but didn't elaborate.

"What about your mother? Is she still alive and smoking?"

"Mom quit smoking after Dad died. She decided she needed to live a healthier lifestyle. She traveled for a while but settled down. She runs a holistic hippie compound about an hour from here for anyone looking to find themselves. They grow their own food, make their own makeshift houses and live a mostly organic if isolated life."

Listening to him talk about his life made Taylor feel as if she were that rabbit in the sky, one that had fallen into another realm. "Really?"

"You think I can make this stuff up?"

"I can't imagine."

"I can take you there sometime."

She'd meant his childhood, but his offer caught her interest. "To meet your mother?"

"To see the compound," he clarified.

Taylor's face heated. She shouldn't have assumed he'd meant anything. "Oh, right. Sorry."

"You'd meet my mom, too, Taylor. She lives there."

"She probably wouldn't like me." The words slipped out of her mouth, revealing way more than what she should have.

"Why's that?"

"Sounds like she's very much a free spirit. That's not who I am. She'd find me plain and boring."

He rolled over onto his side to look at her. "She'd feel you were a kindred soul just waiting to break free from the confines of society and embrace your inner self."

His assumption pleased Taylor more than it should.

"That sounded rehearsed," she accused playfully, giving him a suspicious brow raise.

"You think?" He laughed. "I may have heard her say that a few times."

"About women you've taken to the compound?"

His gaze met hers and he shook his head. "I've never taken a woman to the compound."

"Oh." She stared into his eyes, marveling at how they perfectly matched the sky. "But you'd take me?"

He nodded.

She marveled at his answer, too. "Why?"

"Because you wanted to go. And for the record, you, Taylor, are the least plain and boring person I know."

Although Jack was enjoying lying on the blanket with Taylor, he was ready for a subject change.

"What about your parents? Are they alive? Do they live in Louisville?"

"They are alive. I used to see them a few times a year, but not since my divorce."

The pain in her voice gave any explanation needed. Her parents hadn't approved of her divorce. Had they cut her out of their lives? Or had she had to walk away from them along with her ex?

"I'm sorry."

Her voice breaking, she explained, "They thought I should stay with Neil. In their eyes, I should have appreciated how lucky I was to be married to a successful doctor no matter what he did."

"If you felt the need to leave, your parents should have helped you pack." And her dad should have kicked the guy's tail. Jack reached for her hand and gave it a squeeze. "What did he do?"

Taking a very deep breath, she shrugged. "He was himself. I just didn't see the real him until it was too late and I'd married him." She exhaled sharply. "I was a possession, meant to do as he said when he said, and should have been okay with his infidelity, among other things."

Jack winced. "He cheated on you?"

"Several times that I know of and who knows how many I never learned of?"

"He was an idiot."

Taylor laughed, but there was no pleasure in the sound. "Actually, he's a brilliant plastic surgeon and apparently does amazing work."

Something in her tone told its own tale. "He never operated on you?"

She glanced down at her moderate-sized chest. "Do these appear enhanced to you?"

Jack glanced at her breasts and fought gulping. "I found—find—your breasts just right."

Taylor snorted. "Well, he didn't and wanted to lift and enlarge them. He also offered to pad my bottom and freeze the fat in my thighs and make my nose smaller and my lips fuller and make my chin not so boxy and—"

Jack's finger went over her lips, stopping her words. "You're perfect the way you are, Taylor. He was the one who had problems. Not you. I'm glad you never let him take a knife to you."

Taylor sighed. "Sorry, I got on a rant, didn't I?"

"You deserve to rant. If a woman is unhappy with her body and wants to make changes, that's her choice and more power to her. So long as she is making the change for herself. But a man pushing a woman to change?" He shook his head. "A man should never make a woman feel she needs to make those changes because she's not good enough." He lifted her hand and pressed a kiss there. "You are good enough, Taylor. Way better than he ever deserved."

Better than Jack deserved, too.

"Sometimes I wonder if you're for real," she mused, eyeing him as if she thought he might disappear any moment.

Not sure what she meant, he waited for her to elaborate.

"You seem to know what to say to make me feel better about myself, to be justified in my outrage." She shrugged. "You make me feel better inside, Jack. Thank you for that."

Her compliment made him feel better inside, too. She made him feel better.

"You're welcome." He wasn't sure what else to say. He knew what he wanted to do. He wanted to hold her, kiss her, make love to her right here on a blanket in the middle of nowhere with a babbling little waterfall in the background.

But he'd told her she had the power, that he wouldn't push or do anything until she gave the word it was what she wanted. He wouldn't force himself on Taylor in any way.

So he settled for holding her hand and consoled himself that lying on this blanket, holding her hand in his, was more precious than all the kisses in the world from anyone else.

Which slapped him in the face yet again with the reality of how she affected him.

Taylor had been suppressed her whole life and had never been given the opportunity to just be. Whereas he'd grown up with no boundaries, with parents who'd encouraged him to step outside society lines, she'd been stuffed inside the box of others' expectations and forced to stay within those tight confines.

That she had so newly torn free of that box made her vulnerable, made making sure he did nothing to cause her to stumble and possible fall back into those confines all the more important.

For the next month he intended to help her rip down as many of those walls as possible. To show her the world from his perspective.

After his time was up in Warrenville, well, he hoped when she thought of him, she would smile and feel he'd made her world a little brighter place.

Taylor fiddled with her keys outside Amy's apartment door. "Thank you for today."

"You're welcome."

She'd had an amazing day. The best. Playing in water, cloud watching, a picnic, and then he'd taken her to a Japanese hibachi grill for a late sushi dinner, something else she'd never tried. The day had been filled with laughter, adventure, and light-heartedness.

"Will I see you tomorrow?" she asked.

"Do you want to see me tomorrow?"

He had to know she did. How could she not when their day had been so carefree? Making her feel as if she'd traveled back in time to play with him as part of his childhood?

What she was feeling for him was very grown up.

Very adult.

"Then you'll see me." He winked, much as he had on the nights he'd gone back to his tent, then left.

* * *

An hour later, as Taylor lay in bed, she stared at her ceiling in the darkness of her room, restless, mind racing, heart full.

Sleep wouldn't come.

No matter how long she lay there, she knew it was useless to keep trying.

Because she burned inside.

Burned that she'd not invited Jack inside the apartment. Burned with regret that she'd not invited Jack into her bed.

She wanted him.

Maybe she'd always want him.

He was that kind of man. Strong and virile, yet gentle and patient in a way that made her feel feminine and safe.

Safe.

Sweet, free-spirited Jack.

Inhaling sharply, she fluffed her pillow and rolled over. Calling him safe seemed hypocritical because it was the danger posed by him that had held her back when she'd first moved to Warrenville. That and not wanting him to feel obligated to continue being interested in her. More than anything, she realized she'd been afraid to risk falling in love with Jack.

Jack. Jack. Jack.

She couldn't let herself love him, but she couldn't help but want him.

CHAPTER TWELVE

"Did I wake you?" Jack asked, glancing at his fitness watch to make sure it wasn't earlier than he'd thought.

"Hmm, maybe," came Taylor's response. Sleep had her voice low and raspy over the phone line. Had him envisioning what she must look like and how he'd rather have wakened her.

"I'd ask if you had a late night, but I know what time I dropped you off," he mused.

"Needed my…" she yawned "…beauty sleep."

"Is that how you always look so amazing? Sleep?"

"Listen to you, Mr. Flatterer."

She was starting to sound more awake. An image of her stretching her body flashed into his head and he knew it's what she was currently doing. Arching her back and stretching her arms high above her head.

"It's after ten. I was going to invite you to lunch, but maybe I should call it brunch?"

"Brunch sounds good."

He could hear movement in the background, so she must have gotten out of bed.

"Ouch!" She let loose with a string of expletives that were so mild Jack fought not to laugh.

"We are going to have to enroll you in Cursing for Beginners because that was weak, lady."

"Yeah, well, I wouldn't be a lady if it was too brash, now, would I?" she shot back, eliciting another laugh from him.

"What happened?"

"I stubbed my toe against the coffee-table leg."

The coffee table?

"You were asleep on the sofa?"

"Mmm-hmm. I was too tired to make it to my bed."

"Our hike exhausted you that much yesterday evening?"

"Our hike was wonderful." She yawned again. "Let me shower, then I'll meet you somewhere for that brunch you mentioned. I'm starved."

"Okay if I just pick you up and we'll go together?"

She hesitated a moment, then, "Sure. Give me thirty minutes."

Thirty minutes. He could do that.

"Wear a bathing suit under your clothes."

"Huh?"

He could picture her baffled look.

"No questions. Just go with it."

"We going back to the creek?"

They'd had fun in the creek, but had never gotten into water any deeper than knee-high. He had something different in mind.

Smiling, he promised, "You'll see."

A knock at her apartment door.

She grabbed a big floppy bag into which she'd put her sunscreen, lip balm, cellphone, an extra set of clothes, and keys, and stepped out of the apartment.

Running his gaze over her, Jack whistled. "You must sleep a lot."

Confused, she furrowed her forehead.

"You truly are beautiful and if it's sleep…"

"Ah, I get your drift." She shot him a wry look. "For the record, I would have gotten more except someone called and woke me up this morning."

Spotting Jessica, she stopped walking and turned to look at him, eyes huge. "What are those?"

He grinned. "Kayaks."

"Kayaks?"

"I borrowed them and the trailer from Jeff." When she still looked clueless, he added, "He works in the lab."

Ah, that Jeff.

She continued to stare at Jack a bit in awe. "As in borrowed for us to get in and float around?"

He chuckled. "That's the idea so don't go all *Titanic* on me."

"Kayaking," she mused. "That'll be another first for me." Climbing into Jessica, she exhaled a deep breath. "Hope I don't ruin your day by totally screwing this up. I mean, I won't purposely *Titanic* Jeff's kayak, but what if I accidentally sink it? I've never been into sports or athletic kind of things. If this requires skills of any type, I'm going to disappoint you."

"The only way you'll disappoint me is if you let the voices in your head keep you from giving this a go," he told her. "I enjoy watching you do new things, showing and teaching you new things." He stood next to the passenger side of the Jeep, brushed his hand over her cheek and grinned at her. "Besides, I'm not worried. You've got this."

Jack really was good for her, so nurturing and positive. She'd been trying new things since her divorce but being with Jack made those new experiences seem like baby steps. Then again, she'd had to start somewhere, and baby steps had been huge at the time.

She flashed a big smile that she hoped conveyed how much she appreciated him, then ordered, "Get in Jessica, Jack. You promised brunch and I'm dying of hunger."

Laughing, Jack got in the Jeep.

"That was amazing!" Taylor gushed as she helped pull her kayak out of the river. They'd driven about thirty miles to a rather rundown-looking shack where they'd loaded up their kayaks and themselves on an equally rundown-looking bus without air-conditioning. Kayaks strapped down on top, the bus carried them, along with a dozen others, upstream and dropped them off for them to make their way back to the base where they'd started.

"You know I'm going to want to go again," she continued, amazed at how good her body felt, how good she felt.

Exhilarated. That was it. She felt exhilarated.

"I'm counting on it," Jack assured her, winking at her before turning his attention back to the kayak.

She glanced toward where he'd repositioned her kayak on the bank and tingles of awareness hit as she took in his baggy wet shorts, life jacket that covered a sleeveless T-shirt that had to be plastered to his chest, and a backward-facing baseball cap on top of his head to semi-contain his hair that curled and snaked to just past his shoulders. A scruffy shadow beard shadowed his face.

His arm muscles bulged as he gave the kayak one last tug forward.

When he turned toward her, Taylor didn't attempt to hide her thoughts. She doubted she was that good an actress anyway.

The blue of his eyes darkened as he stared into hers. So much emotion in those depths. So much everything, she thought.

His brow lifted in question.

She'd already been caught and wasn't sure she cared that she had been. Lowering her gaze, she slowly took in all of him. From the width of his shoulders to the scrumptious chest hidden beneath his life jacket, to his narrow waist, hairy legs, and water-shoe-clad feet.

Sexiest river rat she'd ever seen.

A small smile twisted her lips as she met his eyes again.

"Whatever you're thinking, hold that thought forever," he ordered, his dimples dug deep into his cheeks.

Forever?

She hoped not.

But for the next month before he left for new adventures, yeah, she just might.

* * *

"Where are you staying while you're in Warren-ville?" Taylor asked as they finished packing up their kayaks on the small trailer he pulled be-hind Jessica.

Jack made sure the straps holding the kayaks in place were properly tightened, then glanced up. "I've rented a farmhouse a few miles from the hospital. It's too big for one person but was furnished and available for a few months while the deceased estate is settled so it works. Plus, I like the wide open space."

"Oh?"

"Nothing around but rolling hills, farmland, and cows with a few barns, silos, and far-off neighbors. Once the estate is settled, the house and personal property will be auctioned off. At least, that's the plan of the former owner's chil-dren who inherited the place. I don't think they'll have any problems. It's several acres and has a nicely stocked pond for fishing."

"Fishing?"

He arched a brow. "Something else you've not done?"

"I wasn't hinting for you to take me," she said, looking cute in her braids and wet clothes.

Cute? Not exactly the right adjective to de-scribe a woman as naturally beautiful as the one who'd barely been able to contain her enthusiasm during their ride down the river.

"I didn't mean to imply that you were, but I'd gladly take you fishing, Taylor. Just say when."

"Soon," she replied, glancing around to make sure they had everything packed and nothing remained on the gravelly ground.

"I look forward to it," he assured her, walking around the trailer to where she stood. "I had a great time today."

She grinned up at him. "Even though I lost my paddle and you had to tow me until we caught up with it?"

Jack's fingers itched to brush the tiny stray hairs back away from her face, to bend down to kiss her pert pink lips.

He cleared his throat, then said, "I'm just grateful that tree branch was low enough to snag it or I'd have been towing you the whole way."

Not that either of them had had to do a lot of paddling as the current had been good on most of the river with only a few areas where they could idly float.

"Yeah, so was I until you teased me to watch out for snakes on low-lying branches."

He chuckled. "Hungry?"

"Starved."

He'd packed snacks for them on their river ride, but breakfast had been a long time ago and they'd burned off the energy from their snacks hours ago.

"Want to see the farmhouse? I have steaks in the fridge I could grill for us."

Surprise lit her face. "Seriously?"

Not sure why she'd question his invitation, he asked, "Something wrong with steaks? I know you eat meat because I've seen you."

"No, not that. I just meant us going to your place for you to cook for me. It seems..." she shrugged "...such a normal thing to do."

He laughed. "Normal? Are you implying we don't usually do normal?"

"Nothing about what I do with you is normal, Jack."

"I'll take that as a compliment."

"It's meant as one and, yes, steaks sound delicious. I like mine medium to medium-well done. Please and thank you."

Jake's rented farmhouse was like something straight out of a picture book. An old but well-maintained white siding house with a navy roof, shutters, and trim work rested down a gravel road that was fenced on both sides. Cows dotted the pasture on both sides and to the left was the pond Jack must have been referring to.

The family must still have the land farmed because corn grew off in the distance as did some other crop. Taylor wasn't sure what it was. Soybeans, perhaps.

"Like it?" he asked as he pulled to a stop in front of a porch that sprawled all the way across the front of the house. A half-dozen rocking chairs were painted to match the house's navy roof and welcomed any visitor who wanted to spend time rocking away their cares.

Taylor loved it all. Warm, inviting, functional, like it had belonged here a hundred years and would be here another hundred.

"What's not to like?"

"If I ever settled down, I'd want it to be somewhere like here," Jack mused, glancing around the place with obvious admiration.

Taylor's gaze cut toward him.

"Mountains less than an hour away for climbing and hiking," he continued a bit wistfully. "Lots of lakes for skiing and swimming. Rivers and streams everywhere you look. Caves for exploring. Green in the spring and summer and amazing colors covering the hills in the fall. Snow in the winter for sledding and skiing in the mountains."

"I take it you like Tennessee."

He grinned. "Between all the big music festivals in Nashville, Memphis, Chattanooga, Knoxville, and the one in Warrenville, I end up spending most of my summers here, especially now that my mom is in Tennessee permanently."

Such a strange life he led. "Where is home, Jack?"

He shrugged. "Some music festival far, far away."

"An actual place?"

He shook his head. "Not really. Just a metaphorical locale that represents all the different places that made up my childhood."

"You never lived in one place that feels like going home when you visit?"

"Only time I ever lived in one place more than a few months was the year I stayed with my grandparents." He didn't look pleased about the experience.

"You lived with your grandparents?"

"A torturous half-year until everyone realized how miserable I was, being stuck in the same four walls all the time."

She couldn't imagine four walls containing Jack.

"At first, they put it down to me needing to adjust to the change, but I inherited their need to be on the move. Eventually, they realized their mistake and had me back on the road with them."

Whereas her parents lived in the same house they'd moved into when they'd got married and would likely live there until they died. She wasn't sure they'd ever left her hometown other than to attend her graduation from college. Even then, they'd not stuck around but had driven back home that very night, rather than sightseeing or spending time with her.

They were happy, content with their lives, so she didn't begrudge them what worked for them.

It just wasn't the life for her.

As the thought entered her head, Taylor smiled that she'd moved away from everything she'd known other than Amy, that she'd sought a new adventure, that she was living a different life.

Her life.

Mostly she was grateful for Jack because he was the greatest adventure she'd ever encountered.

"Come on," he said, climbing out of the Jeep. "Let's get the grill fired up."

Taylor's clothes had mostly dried on the ride to Jack's farmhouse. But she felt grungy and when he refused to let her help, saying he wanted to do this for her as repayment for the night she'd cooked for him, she asked to take a quick shower.

"You naked in my tub?" he asked, then, grinning, asked, "You think I'm going to say no?"

Rolling her eyes, she asked him to point her in the right direction.

"Better yet, I'll show you."

* * *

Having already placed his steak away from the flame, Jack turned skewered vegetables on the grill next to Taylor's steak.

When she came to the backyard to find him, he glanced up.

She'd left her hair in her double braids and had changed into a different pair of shorts and tank top from the ones she'd kayaked in earlier. Her skin glowed a rosy pink, hopefully from her shower and not from too much sun. Her eyes sparkled, and her expression was soft, relaxed.

Relaxed looked good on Taylor.

Like it belonged, and she should wear it more often.

The back of the house had a patio and grill and if he cooked, it was usually there. Other than a few friends from work and Duffy a few days prior to Rockin' Tyme, he'd never had company at the farmhouse.

"Something smells good," she said, coming close to peek at the food on the grill.

"Yes, you do," he offered.

"Ha, I probably smell like you because I used your bath wash."

Lucky bath wash.

"Positive I've never smelled as good as you. This is almost done."

"Yay. Something about being around you makes me hungry."

"I know the feeling."

Her gaze lifted to his and she smiled. "Oh?"

He nodded. "Being around you increases my appetite, too."

"Um…guess we're both just hungry people around each other, huh?"

"Apparently." Jack cut into one of the steaks, making sure it was cooked somewhere between medium and medium–well done. "Perfect."

"Unlike your raw one there." She crinkled her nose.

Placing her steak on a plate, Jack laughed. "It's called rare, not raw."

She gestured to his steak. "Same difference, apparently."

He put his sirloin on a plate then put a vegetable skewer apiece on the plates. "Dinner is served."

CHAPTER THIRTEEN

"I ATE TOO MUCH," Taylor said, rubbing her belly. They'd cleared their dishes and had gone back outside to sit on the front porch.

She was sure Jack would have gone back outside, but she'd wanted to sit on the front porch. It had been so inviting. She wanted to rock.

So she rocked.

Jack was in the chair beside her but seemed more interested in watching her than in rocking his chair.

"Everything was really good, though," she continued, not content to sit in silence. Surprising because she felt sure she could while away many hours on this porch and feel at peace, but at the moment silence toyed with her sanity.

When he still didn't say anything, she frowned. "Jack, talk to me."

"I'm listening."

"Not the same thing as talking. It takes two to have a conversation."

"What do you want to talk about?"

Ugh. Why did he have to ask her that? And what was she supposed to say?

"Who's Courtney?" She wasn't sure where the question had come from, but somewhere in the recesses of her brain, the name Duffy had thrown at Jack had been agitating her, refusing to go away.

If she'd thought the silence had been thick before, it was nothing compared to the current heaviness of quiet.

"Jack?"

"My girlfriend when I was seventeen."

Okay. Not necessarily what she'd been expecting him to give as his answer. Why would Duffy have brought up a girlfriend from more than a decade ago?

"She had long black hair, the bluest eyes you've ever seen, and I was convinced gravity itself couldn't hold her down she was such a free soul."

Ugh. She did not want to feel jealous of his teenage girlfriend yet listening to Jack describe her, hearing the admiration in his voice, green filled her veins.

"She sounds beautiful." And Taylor's voice sounded envious.

"She was."

Was. Heaviness fell on Taylor's chest. Was. Did that mean…?

"I fell in love with her before I even knew her name." Jack sounded far away. "When she told me her name was Courtney, I knew she had to be lying because I'd have guessed Star or Rain or Cloud or Petal or something equally earthy, you know?"

She didn't, of course, but he wouldn't have heard her answer either way because he wasn't with her. Memories of a woman he'd loved had hold of him, and he was far away.

"When I finally found my voice I told her as much. She laughed and told me I could call her anything I wanted. I told her my name, and with that carefree laugh she had she said, 'Okay, Jack.' I was sixteen at the time and she was eighteen. Age didn't matter. Just being with her."

His eyes closed and he paused a moment, seeming lost in his memories.

"She'd run away from home years before and had been working music festivals for cash ever since. Sometimes parking cars during the daytime, sometimes working food booths, sometimes doing Lord only knows what to make ends meet." A short spurt of air came from his pursed lips. "I grew up around drugs and free-living, and was no saint, but Courtney got mixed up with some things better left alone. She hid it from me at first, but soon enough I saw the highs, the lows when she needed a fix. I hated it but was so in love with her I'd have done anything for her."

Taylor wasn't sure she wanted to hear more yet waited with bated breath for him to continue.

"We had been at a music fest in California for a couple of days and had another night to go. I was seventeen, almost eighteen by then. She was living hard. I don't know where she got the drugs, how she afforded them or what she did to get them. Like I said, I didn't want to know," he admitted. "One minute we were dancing and living what I thought was the greatest life ever and the next she fell at my feet and never woke up again."

"Oh, Jack. I'm sorry." She was. Sorry for the pain she heard in his voice.

"We had argued about how much she was using on occasion, but she wouldn't quit. Don't get me wrong, I was using stuff better left alone myself, but even so I could see the dangerous tightrope she was walking. I should have made her get help. Instead, I was as addicted to her as she was to her next high, so I turned a blind eye. In the long run, it cost me her." With tortured eyes, his gaze met hers. "I should have saved her, but I didn't."

"You know as well as I do that a person has to want to get help, Jack. You can't make someone overcome an addiction."

"Logically, I know that. But my seventeen-year-old heart has never believed it."

"I know you, Jack. If you could have helped her, you would have."

"It's where I met Duffy, you know."

She hadn't but waited for him to continue.

"I figured she'd just partied too hard and would sleep it off. But something inside me told me more was going on. I picked her up and carried her to the medical tent, praying she had just passed out and wasn't in any real danger, that she wouldn't kill me for telling the medics she'd possibly overdosed and wasn't picky about how she got her high. She crashed within a minute of me getting her to the medical tent. They tried to save her. Duffy and another man, a doctor, but she…was gone."

Taylor's heart hurt. She reached across the space between their chairs and took his hand. "Oh, Jack."

He sucked in a breath. "It was the first I'd met him, but Duffy spent a lot of time with me that night. I think he thought I was going to hurt myself and was afraid no one else would keep a constant eye on me. He never let me out of his sight. Not even when I went to the john."

He gave a humorless snort.

"I don't think I would have done anything, but I wasn't in my head that night. I was coming down off my own high and the light that lit my world had just gone out."

He swallowed hard.

"I didn't know who her family was, just her name. Duffy helped track them down, but no one came for her body. No one seemed to care that she was gone. Maybe that's why she'd left to begin with." He sighed. "Somehow, Duffy arranged for her to be cremated or maybe it was the State of California who did that. I don't know, just that Duffy was there and helped get her ashes for me. He saved me."

Fighting tears, Taylor squeezed his hand. "I'm glad he was there."

"Me, too." Jack swiped at his eyes, swallowed hard, then exhaled. "I'm not sure what would have happened to me had he not been working that night and taken a kid under his wing."

"You'd have found your way."

"Maybe, but I could have just as easily have slipped off that slippery slope that had claimed Courtney. Like I said, I was using myself."

"Instead," she reminded him, "you became a doctor."

"Because I became a doctor," he clarified. "I watched Duffy and that doctor work on Courtney, trying to save her life, and I knew that's what I had to do. I wanted to save lives, to make a difference to someone someday, the way they'd tried to make a difference for her and did make a difference for me."

Taylor's heart swelled at what Jack had gone through, at how something so devastating had not pulled him down but had lifted him up to become the man before her.

"You're a good person, Jack."

He snorted. "I've done some things that weren't so good during my life."

"Most people have."

Jack wondered if Taylor ever had. She was a good, decent person. He couldn't imagine her ever having done anything truly bad.

"I'm glad you stayed in touch with Duffy."

"Stayed in touch?" Jack scoffed. "He wouldn't leave me alone. He made me his pet project or the son he never had or whatever he likes to call it. Regardless, he has been there at every major life event since. University graduation, and then med school. And—" she'd think him crazy "—a few years ago he went with me to scatter Courtney's ashes."

He could tell by her face that she wondered what he'd done with them. It had taken him years to let them go, years to figure out where.

"We flew to Hawaii, hired a guide, went to the top of a volcano, and tossed her in."

Taylor's eyes widened. "What?"

It probably did seem crazy, but he had no regrets. Not for that.

"For years I tried to figure out where she'd want to be scattered. Almost threw her over a ledge into the Grand Canyon once, but it didn't feel right." He shrugged, then half smiled. "Being thrown into a volcano, that she would not only have approved of but she'd have loved it."

At Taylor's look of uncertainty, he took a deep breath then tried to explain.

"When a volcano blows, bits of ash are scattered through the atmosphere, even thousands of miles away. She'd be everywhere." A peace came over him. "Free, floating above the earth, seeing everything and slowly drifting down to become a part of everything." His voice lowered as he said, "She'd be everywhere. The volcano blew a year or so ago. *She is everywhere.*"

When she spoke, Taylor would probably demand he take her home. He wouldn't blame her. No way could she have anticipated his elaborate answer when she'd asked who Courtney was.

He didn't talk about Courtney.

Never with anyone other than Duffy on the rare occasion. That he so freely spilled out the horrid details to Taylor shook him. Why had he? He could have stopped with his girlfriend from when he'd been seventeen and left it at that. Taylor probably thought him crazy.

He was.

But she hadn't pulled away or demanded he drive her home. Not yet. Instead, Taylor's hand was warm, held his tight. But neither of them spoke for the longest time. He'd already said too much.

"That's a very beautiful tribute, Jack," she finally said. "She must have been a very special person for you to have loved her so much."

"I've never known anyone like her."

"I'm sorry you lost her."

"Me, too." Although, he wondered whether, if Courtney had lived, they'd have lasted or if he'd have tired of her abusing her body with drugs and whatever it took to get them. As much as he'd loved her, the man he was today wouldn't have stayed to watch such self-destructive behavior.

He was all about being a free spirit, but believed life was about a higher purpose, serving others. He liked to think that even had he never met Duffy he'd have found his calling, his purpose.

Knowing Taylor had to be tired of their depressing conversation, he stood from the rocker. "Let's go for a walk."

"In the dark?"

"You afraid?" he challenged, reaching his hand out to pull her up from her chair.

"Should I be?"

"I promised you I'd never let anything hurt you," he reminded her, and meant it. With everything in him he'd do his best to keep Taylor from being hurt.

Taking his hand, she stood from her chair, laced her fingers with his, and said, "Let's walk."

Taylor had lingered out in the cow pasture for as long as she could.

Jack would take her home when they got back to the house.

She didn't want to go back to the apartment.

She wanted to stay here, with Jack. Crazy, but she didn't want to leave him. At the moment she didn't even want to strip him naked and have her way with him—although that was just beneath the surface.

What she wanted was to hold him.

Because Jack needed to be held. When they got back to the house he turned to her. "Is your bag from when you showered still in the house?"

She nodded.

"You want me to get it and us head toward your place?"

No, that wasn't what she wanted.

"I can get it." She could. "But if you want to grab it for me, that would be great. I left it in the living room."

"Be back in just a few."

Taylor watched him go inside, then took off after him, berating herself with each step. She was making a habit of following this man in hopes of ending up in his bed.

Only this time sex wasn't her sole motivating factor.

Hearing Taylor enter the house behind him, Jack turned toward her. He'd just spotted her bag on the living room sofa and was about to pick it up.

"I'm not leaving." She stared him straight in the eyes.

He arched his brow. "You're not?"

She shook her head. "I'm staying with you tonight. Here." Her chin lifted as if she thought he might defy her. "I want to sleep next to you and hold you and wake up with you."

Jack swallowed to moisten his dry throat. "Is that all?"

"For the moment."

Jack wasn't sure he was a strong enough man to sleep next to Taylor with her holding him and that was all. He felt as if he'd wanted her forever. As if it had been forever since he'd touched her, kissed her, shared his air mattress with her for a few magical hours.

"Okay."

His agreeing with her seemed to knock some

of the wind out of her sails, because uncertainty flashed into her eyes. Whatever, she quickly masked it and smiled.

"Good answer."

"It wasn't as if I was going to refuse you saying you want to spend the night in my bed."

"Perfect." She smiled, then gave him a little *come hither* look. "I'm going to get ready for bed."

Jack glanced at his fitness band. "It is getting late, isn't it?"

Taylor yawned and he laughed.

She didn't have a clue how beautiful she was.

"You have a twinkle in your eyes, Taylor Hall."

Her lips twitched. "A twinkle?"

"Like the prettiest star in the night sky."

Eyes sparkling, she gave him a dubious look. "That's a big claim because you and I just saw some amazing stars."

"Not nearly as amazing as looking into your eyes."

She laughed, and it was a sound of pure merriment. "On that full-of-it note, get me a big, comfy T-shirt to sleep in, please."

Taylor followed him into his room. Opening a chest of drawers, he pulled out the top T-shirt, not surprised when it was a music festival one. He kept his wardrobe simple. "This work?"

Taking it, she ran her fingers over the soft cotton material. "I think so. Thanks. Okay if I use the bathroom first and borrow your toothbrush?"

He nodded. He'd just jump in the shower across the hallway while she got ready for bed. He probably smelled like a cross between grill smoke, river water, and cow pasture. Not the scent he wanted to wear to bed with Taylor.

Taylor had meant to hurry in the bath, but she'd heard the hot water heater kick on and knew Jack was showering somewhere in the house.

Staring into his bathroom mirror, she studied her reflection. What was she doing?

Staying with Jack.

Because Jack made her happy, was a good person, and she wanted to comfort him, to soothe away his sorrows, and give him happiness.

What makes you think you can make him happy? a nagging voice mocked.

She glared at her image, as if the voice had come directly from her reflection.

"Just watch me and find out," she whispered, then stripped out of her clothes, all her clothes, and stood naked in Jack's bathroom.

She took a cloth and washed herself, then helped herself to some unscented body lotion. She brushed her teeth and slipped on his T-shirt.

It fell to just beneath her hips, covering her bottom, but just barely.

Perfect.

Reaching up, she touched a braid. If she left them in, her hair wouldn't be nearly so everywhere in the morning.

But she wanted her hair loose, not confined, and began the painstaking task of undoing her braids.

When she'd finished, she fingered-combed out her wavy hair. Wild. Crazy. Free.

Perfect.

Because tonight she was going to be wild, crazy, and free.

With Jack.

"You okay in there?"

Cheeks flushing at her thoughts and that she'd taken so long he'd felt the need to check on her, she called, "Fine."

Opening the bathroom door, she almost bumped into him as he stood just on the other side.

"Oh!"

He caught her shoulders, steadying her.

In her bare feet, he seemed so much taller and she looked up at him, smiled. "Thanks."

"You're welcome." He brushed his palms down her arms. "Since you were woken up so bright and early, I suppose you want to hit the sack immediately."

She glanced behind him at the big wooden bed with its antique-appearing quilt on top. "Hope that's okay."

"Anything you want." But he didn't move toward the bed, or at all.

"Kiss me," she ordered, staring up at him to watch the emotions play across his handsome face.

"Taylor—" he began.

"Kiss me, Jack. You said anything I want. I want you to kiss me."

Heaven help him, Jack thought. Or just heaven. Because pressing his lips to Taylor's, tasting her sweetness, was heaven.

"What else do you want?" he asked, lifting his mouth millimeters from hers.

She placed her hands on each side of his face. "You, Jack. I want you. I want you to kiss me, to touch me, to hold me and caress me and make love to me in that big old bed over there, and then I want to sleep in your arms. Is that okay?"

He shook his head, causing concern to fill her pretty brown eyes.

"It would be a travesty to label all that as just okay, Taylor. Okay means mediocre. Nothing about you in my bed would be mediocre."

Her lips curved into a smile, then she stood on tiptoe and kissed him.

Jack could no longer keep his hands still. He traced them over her arms, down her spine, her waist, cupped her bottom.

That's when he realized.

Pulling back, he stared into her eyes. "You're not wearing underwear."

She gave him a devilishly seductive look. "Is that a problem?"

Slowly, he shook his head, then slipped his hands beneath the T-shirt hem to palm her bare bottom. Yeah, it would be easy to just strip off his clothes and push her down on the bed and take her as quickly as she'd let him inside. But that urgency was what had happened last time. This time he wanted to see her, touch her, taste her—all of her.

That's what he set about doing.

Jack's mouth was driving Taylor insane. Absolutely mental.

She dug her fingers into his long hair, loving the luscious slightly damp locks between her fingers, around her hands. She arched against him. "Jack."

"Hmm?" He glanced up at her.

"Just Jack."

Her entire body hummed for him, every cell

trying to draw nearer, to be the part touching him, being touched by him.

Over and over he brought her to the brink, letting her climax, float partially down, then lifting her back up, higher and higher each time.

Digging her heels into the bed, she tugged on his shoulders. "Now, Jack. Now," she demanded. "I need you now."

Within seconds he was above her, donning a condom, then inside her, stretching her in the sweetest way.

With the first movement of his body her insides trembled, then went full-blown earthquake.

She clung to him, hanging on because she was sure she was falling from some other world as he continued to move, continued to take her places she'd only dreamed of.

Momentum built, and she felt his waning willpower to hold back. Needing to feel his loss of control, to feel him give in to the magic between their bodies, she met him stroke for stroke, deeper and deeper.

"Jack!" she cried, realizing she was going to be the one to go tumbling over into orgasmic release yet again.

She reached the pinnacle, the highest place she'd ever been, and plummeted over to the other side, her entire body imploding into a colorful meltdown.

Which undid Jack and he followed suit, driving deep into her body before collapsing onto her.

CHAPTER FOURTEEN

TAYLOR DIDN'T RECALL a month having ever gone by so quickly. Not ever.

The past one had flown and, with it, Jack's days in Warrenville.

Eight days. Then he'd be gone.

"You've still not talked to him, have you?"

Sitting in their living room, Taylor glanced over at Amy, started to pretend she didn't know what her roommate meant, but decided against it. Why bother? Amy knew what was in her heart.

She shook her head.

"You need to tell him you don't want him to go," Amy advised, moving to the sofa to sit next to Taylor. "Tonight, before any more time gets away, before he gets away."

It wasn't that Taylor didn't want to tell Jack that she didn't want him to leave. She didn't want him to leave and wanted to tell him.

But she couldn't ask him to stay.

Every time she thought about doing so memories of how he'd described living at his grandparents' echoed through her head. Jack was a free spirit, not meant to be confined to one place. So, instead of defending why she hadn't, and wouldn't, ask Jack to stay, she went on the offensive.

"How about you? Have you talked to Greg about how this long-distance thing is wearing thin? Have you asked him about opening a practice in Warrenville?"

"I know what you're doing, and it isn't going to work," Amy warned.

"Neither would asking Jack to stay."

"You don't know that."

Amy was right. She didn't know that. She saw how he looked at her, felt how he touched her. He might say yes. But asking Jack to stay would be like asking a bird to give up flying to live in a cage.

How did one ask that of someone they cared for?

She did care for Jack. Way too much. How could she not when he made her laugh, made her feel things she hadn't known possible, made her step beyond the ordinary lines of her life?

A knock sounded at the door.

"Speaking of the lucky devil," Amy said, motioning to the door. "I should get that and tell him myself."

Jumping off the sofa, Taylor's eyes widened. "Don't."

Amy took on a pouty look. "You know I wouldn't really, but I think you should."

"Trust me, I shouldn't."

Sighing, Amy shrugged. "If you say so. You'd better let him in."

Taylor nodded. "He's taking me frog-gigging."

"He's what?" Amy looked disgusted. "I take it back. Let him go."

But her friend was teasing and they both knew it.

After they spotted the first frog, Taylor was done. No way did she want to participate in spearing a frog. Just the thought of Jack killing the frog had her turning to wade back out of the water. Loudly, and with as much splashing noise as she could make.

Hop away, froggy. Hop away.

"I'm all for learning new things," she told Jack, hoping her sloshing feet scared the frog away. She hoped it did, and that it sent all the neighboring frogs into hiding. "But you're on your own with this one. I want no part of murdering frogs."

Following her rather than going after the frog, Jack laughed and asked, "Not your thing?"

She shook her head. "If you want to feed me

frog legs, I can't have seen those legs still attached to a body with eyes that looked at me," she warned.

He chuckled. "Fair enough. I brought fishing poles so if we didn't find any frogs we wouldn't get bored."

Fishing didn't bother her. Jack mostly was a catch and release fisherman, only keeping what he planned to eat.

"Fishing in the dark?"

He'd taken her fishing, several times in fact, but never at night. Just the weekend before they'd gone out with friends, including Greg and Amy, on a nearby lake and whiled the day away with water-skiing, tubing, fishing, and soaking up sunshine. That evening they'd had a fish-fry at Jack's and had all sat around eating, laughing. It had been a perfect day.

Every day with Jack was a perfect day.

"Some of my best fishing has been at night."

In the moonlight, she looked at him a little in awe. "Is there anything you can't do, Jack?"

He got quiet, then shrugged. "Lots, but I'll try most things once."

Such as living in one place. He'd tried that once. He'd been miserable. He'd said so himself. Who was she to try to force that on him again?

"I know what you're thinking, Taylor."

He did? Her eyes were probably bigger than the full moon shining down on them.

"I keep thinking about it, too."

She blinked. He was?

"Eight days isn't long enough."

Taylor's breath caught. Was he going to stay longer? And what if he did? She kept thinking about him, about how he was a free spirit, but what about her? She'd had no plans to wrap her life around a man, to get so wrapped up in a man that, rather than focusing on learning who she was, she focused on him. Her plans were to build a career, to get to know herself, her likes and dislikes, to do the things that made her happy. Not to add a man to the equation who she felt she had to cater to.

Jack gave a heartfelt sigh. "But it will have to be."

She wanted him to stay, yet maybe, for her own sake, his leaving was best all the way around.

They ended up not doing much fishing but made love on a blanket spread near his pond. The moonlight created the perfect hue. Taylor didn't ask him to stay, not with her mouth. That she kept quiet. Her brain said he needed to go for, oh, so many reasons.

Her body, however, had a mind of its own and begged him to be hers forever.

* * *

Tracing a pattern across Jack's chest, Taylor snuggled closer against him.

She'd given up any pretense of going home this last week. Going home was a waste of precious time she could have spent with Jack.

"I can't believe tomorrow is your last day at the hospital," she told him, hoping her voice didn't convey how utterly bereft the thought made her feel. The music festival in Daytona started the following Thursday so she imagined he'd want to arrive on Wednesday to check things out. That left four days.

Four days to make a lifetime of memories.

"You going to miss me?"

"A little," she answered with false bravado.

He laughed. "Good to know where I stand."

She glanced up at him. "You know I'm going to miss you, Jack Morgan. Way more than a little."

Bending his neck toward her, he kissed her forehead.

"I mean, who is going to take me fishing? Or boating? Or hiking? Or skinny-dipping in the pond?"

"We never went skinny-dipping in the pond."

"No?" She feigned innocence. "We still have four days."

His body tensed beneath her and she knew whatever he was going to say wasn't good.

"About that…"

Her stomach tightened.

"Duffy called today. We've worked Daytona together for as long as I can remember. Last year, we went down a few days early and scuba-dived at an old shipwreck site. He wants to go out again."

Her heart pounded. "Before the festival?"

Jack nodded.

Taylor scooted back from where she'd been pressed against him and sat up. "How long before the festival?"

"I need to head out the day after tomorrow. He's booked us."

"Why would he book you without checking to make sure it was okay? That you didn't already have plans?" Her voice had a panicked edge. He was leaving. Early.

"Because it's what we've always done, and it's never been a problem. There's never been a reason for me to stay anywhere once a job finished. He knows that."

His words shot arrows into her heart. She'd wondered if he'd told Duffy anything about her, if the older man even knew she was in Warrenville with him, that they'd been together this past month.

That this time Jack had a reason to stay a few days more.

He didn't meet her eyes. "I won't leave Duffy hanging, Taylor."

No, he wouldn't. Part of her understood and didn't want him to. Duffy had been a good part of his life for so long. The kind of friend one rarely found. Jack had to go.

But the selfish part of her wanted every last second with him.

"I know that's not when I'd originally thought I would be leaving."

She didn't say anything, couldn't say anything.

"I'm sorry, Taylor."

"It's okay."

Nope. Not even mediocre.

Jack leaving earlier than planned sucked. She'd thought she had four more days to say goodbye, that they'd work their shift tomorrow, then have tomorrow night and three days of just them.

Instead, she had a little over twenty-four hours, twelve plus of which would be spent at the hospital.

"I started to tell you earlier, but didn't want that hanging over our evening."

"I appreciate that." She almost wished she didn't know now, that he'd just waited until the last minute, said goodbye and left. That way she wouldn't have had to count down those last minutes.

"I hear the hurt in your voice." He touched her face, lifting her chin. "Look at me."

She met his gaze. Barely.

"This past month has been amazing. You've been amazing."

She nodded. *Don't cry. You are not going to cry. No tears, Taylor. No tears.*

"I've never known anyone like you, Taylor Hall."

"Ditto, Jack Morgan." She faked a smile and reminded herself that she'd known this moment would come from the beginning, that he wasn't doing her wrong and that she shouldn't feel hurt. She should be happy for the experiences she'd had with Jack and ready to move on to the next phase of her life.

With the life she'd planned when she'd moved to Warrenville.

Just look at how she'd let a man flub up her plans yet again. She should be glad he was leaving so she could get on with her life.

She should be.

He leaned forward, kissed her forehead. "Thank you, Taylor. For everything."

The emergency department was slammed. A stomach virus had broken out at a nearby nursing-home facility and was running rampant among residents and staff. Due to their already fragile health, several residents had needed to be transported by ambulance for emergency room work-up to see who would be okay with administration of intravenous fluids to rehydrate them then sent back to the facility, and who needed actual admission for closer observation.

Other than with regard to patients, Jack barely got to speak with Taylor.

Which was okay.

They had tonight to say their goodbyes.

He'd never had trouble leaving anywhere, but he'd stayed in Warrenville long enough that he would miss the small Tennessee town.

Would miss Taylor.

One last night to make love to her, to hold her in his arms while she slept, to wake beside her and make love to her all over again.

Only apparently not.

"Taylor is sick in the ladies' room," Amy announced matter-of-factly. "I think she's caught whatever this bug is."

"Is she all right?"

"Other than the fact she lost all her stomach contents in less than three seconds?"

Jack winced. "I'm going to check on her."

Amy's eyes widened. "In the ladies' room?"

"What are they going to do? Fire me?"

"Yeah, I guess they wouldn't bother, with it being your last day and all."

He doubted they would fire him for checking on an ill nurse regardless, but he didn't care. Taylor was sick, and he needed to check on her.

"Make sure there's no one else in there," he ordered Amy. "I'm not worried about being fired, but I wouldn't want to walk in on someone unexpectedly either."

Amy looked skeptical. "Taylor isn't going to like you seeing her this way."

"Then she shouldn't have gotten sick with me being the doctor on duty."

"He's insisting he come in here, Tay."

Struggling to find the energy to lift her head from where it rested on her knees, heavy and throbbing, Taylor squinted at her friend.

Still fighting the nausea racking her body, she grimaced. "Please, no." Her entire body ached, felt wretched. "He leaves tomorrow. This…" she gestured to herself sitting on the bathroom floor "…is not how I want him to remember me."

"He looked intent on checking on you. I'm not sure I can stop him."

"Try."

"Too late."

The last came from Jack.

Rather than look toward him, Taylor lowered

her forehead back to her knees. She wanted to curl into a ball and disappear.

"You were supposed to wait until I gave you the all clear," Amy scolded.

"You were in here long enough I knew Taylor was alone." His voice was growing closer. "Go keep an eye on things out there. If I'm needed, get me."

Nothing, then footsteps, the sound of the door opening and closing.

Amy had abandoned her. She didn't even have the strength to protest.

Jack bent, placed his hand on her back. "Are you hurting?"

Did the excruciating ache in her chest count? Or just the horrific cramps gripping her stomach?

His hand went to her forehead. "You're burning up with fever. How long have you been fighting this?"

Since a few hours after the first nursing-home patient had come in. She'd thought she'd be okay, writing her symptoms off to stress over Jack leaving even as they'd continued to mount throughout her shift. Fifteen minutes ago denial had become impossible.

She rarely got sick. Why today?

"You shouldn't be in here," she said, hearing

the whine in her voice and beyond caring. "I don't want to make you sick, too."

"You won't."

"You're not impervious to germs, Jack."

He sighed. "I can't leave you on the bathroom floor. Let me carry you to one of the bays. I'll give you something to calm your stomach down."

The thought of him picking her up, jostling her around, did not appeal.

"I don't want to move."

He wasn't having it. "You can't stay here indefinitely."

"I don't plan on being sick indefinitely." Her stomach churned, threatening to miraculously produce something more. Impossible. No way could there be anything left. "Please, Jack. Send a shot with Amy, if you must, but let me stay here until it kicks in."

"Won't you look at me?"

"No. I hate you seeing me like this."

"I'm a doctor, Taylor. This is what I do."

"This is not what we do." She hugged her knees even tighter, mentally willing her stomach not to turn inside out in front of him. She felt Jack's tension, his indecision. He wanted to force her to go to the bay, force her to do as he wanted, because he thought it was the right thing. Stubbornly, that made her that more determined to stay. *She* decided what happened to her, not him or any man. Right? Besides, she really didn't want to move.

"If you want me to send Amy back, that's what I'll do."

Stunned he'd agreed, that he hadn't scooped her up and carried her out of the bathroom whether she wanted to go or not, Taylor moved her head in an up-and-down motion or as close as she could get without raising her forehead from her knees.

He didn't sound happy about it when he said, "I'll get Amy."

Jack insisted on helping Taylor to Amy's car. He'd wanted to drive her home, but several of the staff were throwing a going-away party for him in the break room. It wouldn't last long, but he was anxious to leave the entire time he was shaking hands and hugging co-workers he'd genuinely grown to care about.

The main co-worker he cared about had gone home over an hour ago and he wanted to check on her before getting a few hours' sleep, then driving to Daytona to meet up with Duffy.

He didn't call, wouldn't risk being told not to come, just drove to the apartment and knocked on the door.

Amy opened it and shushed him. "She's finally asleep. Don't you wake her up."

His heart fell. "Can I see her?"

Amy looked torn. "I don't think she'd want me to let you."

"But you're going to." Hope glimmered inside and grew as Amy's expression softened.

Amy eyed him, then sighed. "Only because I like you and she's not the only one who's going to miss you."

He'd swear she'd just sniffled.

Jack hugged her. "You'll see me again next summer at Rockin' Tyme. Same time, same place. You know the drill."

She nodded. "Maybe sooner if I can convince Greg to move here."

Jack smiled, hoping things worked out for his friends. "Maybe so."

With care to be as quiet as possible, he pushed Taylor's bedroom door open and made his way to stand beside her bed.

She looked pale, fragile. But he knew better. Knew she was strong and would be okay. Better than okay. Nothing about her was mediocre. Taylor was a butterfly emerging from a lifelong cocoon and was only just beginning to use her wings. He was humbled he'd gotten to be a small part of her learning to take flight, to soar.

"Bye, Taylor. It's been fun," he whispered, so low he doubted it was even audible.

Unable to resist, he stroked his fingers over her hair.

Her eyes opened.

He should feel bad he'd woken her up. She was sick. But he couldn't leave without saying good-bye to her and knew he'd hoped she'd awaken at his touch.

"Shh," he warned. "If Amy finds out I've woken you, she'll skin me alive."

Although obviously still ill, Taylor gave a small semblance of a smile.

"Feeling any better?"

"A little." She glanced toward the night table where Amy had put a cup of ginger ale with a straw. "Please."

Jack held the cup out to her, positioning it so she could sip while he held the cup. She didn't take in much, but at least it was something.

Seeing her so weak, so unlike her normal vibrant self, threatened to undo him. How could he leave until she was back on her feet?

"I'll stay if you need me to. I'll call Duffy and tell him you're sick. He'll understand."

Face pale, she shook her head. "You shouldn't be anywhere near me. I'm contagious."

He took her hand in his, marveling at how

fragile she felt. "You're not the first contagious patient I've been around, Taylor."

She nodded almost imperceptibly.

"Is there anything I can get you?"

She shook her head. "I just feel tired. I want to go to sleep."

Which he'd woken her from.

"I didn't picture our goodbye quite this way." He hesitated, studying her hand within his. "If you ever need me, Taylor, for anything, a new adventure, whatever, you know how to get in touch with me. Always."

But he wasn't sure she heard him, because her eyes had closed, and her breathing evened out in sleep.

"Goodbye," he whispered, marveling at just how much he wanted to stay but knowing he'd stayed in Warrenville longer than he should have already.

It was past time for him to move on to *his* next adventure. So why was it so hard?

Taylor refused to just go through the motions of life. She'd been there, done that with Neil, and during the aftermath of their marriage and subsequent divorce. Had gone through those motions during her childhood with the parents she'd never been able to please, so she'd faded into the background instead. She'd existed without really living. She wouldn't go back.

Not now that she'd gotten a glimpse of what life truly could be.

What she was determined it would be.

She went out dancing. She went to the lake with friends. She found an art class, got access to a kiln, and started a piece, but had started over several times because she'd known it wasn't right, that what she was uncovering wasn't what was really hidden in the clay. She'd even white-water rafted with a group from work. She lived, took chances, was the first to volunteer to try something new. Some she enjoyed, some not so much. Either way, she was discovering what she liked and disliked. It was a good life.

She missed Jack and found herself wishing he was there to share her adventures, to share everything. Oh, how she missed his easy smile and twinkly eyes. Earlier that day, restless, she'd driven out to the farm Jack had rented. A "SOLD" sign had been placed at the end of the drive. Her heart broke a little at the knowledge she'd never sit on the front porch again, or fish in the pond, or make love to Jack in the big antique bed with its hand-stitched quilt.

But life went on without Jack Morgan.

Perhaps not as brightly or as sweet an adventure, but life was good.

If she'd learned nothing else, she'd learned she had control over her attitude and the direction of her life. She refused to let it be bad.

The piece of clay she'd been working on again earlier, however, was a different story. That was bad. In the corner of her bedroom, the box into which she'd packed her supplies called to her as surely as if someone were locked inside and pleaded for her to rescue them.

Unable to resist the siren call any longer, she flipped on the lamp and began carrying her supplies into the living/dining room combo. Within minutes she had a protective plastic cover spread over the small dining-room table and her fingers were covered in clay. Immediately, the wet earth soothed something deep in her soul and she began to pinch away bits of clay, molding and shaping, using her fingers, using picks and wooden sticks to free whatever, whoever was trapped inside the clay.

Herself, she thought. Jack had been right when he'd interpreted the piece she'd given to Amy. It was always her that emerged from the clay.

When she'd originally realized that was what kept happening, Taylor had wondered if her art was much like putting together puzzle pieces of herself, slowly letting who she was come into view, slowly getting back to a whole.

As her hands worked, a smile lifted her cheeks.

She truly felt whole.

Was that why she'd been so hesitant to let Jack in? Because she worried that, much like what she was doing with her clay, he'd slowly pinch away the pieces she'd worked so carefully to put back together? Did she worry he'd bend her and mold her into something different than the woman she was destined to be?

Being with him had felt so good, so liberating, it was difficult for her to imagine him stifling her the way Neil had done. But she'd been blind to Neil's true nature until after they'd married, until she'd experienced his cruelty in bed and life first-hand.

Her hand slipped, and she took off a bigger piece of clay than she'd intended.

Letting out a frustrated huff, she painstakingly added the clay back and worked until it was impossible to tell that anything had ever been missing.

Minutes became an hour. An hour became hours. Night became morning.

She sat. She stood. She moved around the table, leaned forward, stepped back, working on different angles as she slowly chipped away at the clay. Her neck ached and was stiff from how long she'd been working, but she wasn't tired. Her creativity energized her, pushing her forward, refusing to let her leave the table as she worked on intricate details that were taking shape.

When she was finished, she stepped back and eyed the piece.

She wasn't very good, doubted she ever would be even if a new instructor had told her she was a gifted, natural-born sculptor, but what she saw awed her more than a little.

And revealed a lot about where her head was.

Or more specifically her heart.

"Wow, Tay."

At Amy's exclamation, Taylor prised her eyes open, realizing she'd crashed on the living-room sofa, and peered up at where her friend was glancing back and forth between the table and where Taylor lay.

"That," her friend continued, "is amazing and you look like death on a cracker."

Stretching her stiff body, she wiggled into a sitting position. "It's a piece of clay and, thanks, you look great this morning, too."

"Right and the *Mona Lisa* is just a painting."

"Did you just compare my work to the *Mona Lisa*? Wow." Taylor glanced toward what she'd spent most of the night working on. It needed to be bisqued, painted, and glazed still, but pride swelled in her chest as she stared at the piece. She smiled at her best friend. "It's not nearly that spectacular, but it's the best I've ever done by far, so thank you."

"It's amazing." Amy plopped down on the sofa next to her and stared at the piece. "If I could make something like that, you'd better believe I'd give it to Greg."

She didn't bother pretending that she didn't know what her friend meant. She knew. Just as Amy knew. As always, she'd made a piece of herself—but for the first time a part of someone else had emerged from her clay.

She walked over to the table, stared at the piece. It was abstract, but there was no denying the heart overflowing from the hands that held it.

Jack's hands.

Her heart.

Because Jack held her heart.

"Jack is a traveling man with all his worldly belongings fitting in a Jeep. I don't think he'd want to lug this thing around in Jessica."

She thought back to the day she'd gotten sick, the day he'd left, to his words as he'd stood by her bed. She'd pretended to be asleep because she hadn't trusted herself to say another word. She'd needed him to leave before she forgot how he had a wandering soul and how hard she'd worked for her independence and begged him to stay.

Not just until her illness passed, but for forever.

He'd cared for her. She knew he cared. Had she asked him, he might have stayed. But how could she bind him that way when the very essence of him was freedom?

"He's in Chattanooga, you know."

No, she hadn't known. She'd not heard from Jack since he'd left her room that night. Neither had she reached out to him. There had been nothing else to say. She was living the life she wanted, the life she'd worked hard for, and so was he.

Her fingers itched to run over the hands holding her heart. Jack's hands.

Things were as they should be.

Are they? Are they really?

"Just for two days," Amy continued. "He's working a tough-guy competition. Greg is driving down to see him tomorrow and take in some of the action. You should call."

Jack was in Tennessee. An hour from her. Oh, Jack. Just knowing he was near made the air in her chest feel thick, making breathing difficult.

"He knows where I am if he wants to see me."

Her comment to Amy echoed through her head, causing similar words to replay. Words she'd replayed hundreds of times over the past two months.

If she ever needed him, she knew how to get in touch with him.

What if she'd needed him before he'd left? Still needed him? What if she always needed him? What then?

Nothing had changed. Jack was a free spirit. She wouldn't be the one to attempt to shackle him.

She was a woman who had fought hard to win her independence, to find her voice, to find herself, and she wasn't willing to give it up.

"What about you?" Amy asked. "You know where he is. Do you want to see him? Does he know you want to see him?"

She wanted Jack to be happy, not trapped in a white picket fence world with her.

Who says you have to live in a white picket fence world? Or that you even want to?

She'd been raised to think that was what she wanted, needed, but hadn't she learned to think for herself long ago? Hadn't she put aside others' expectations to discover what her *own* expectations from life were?

Her gaze cut to Amy's. "Who says I even want to live in a white picket fence world? To live a normal nine-to-five life?"

"Huh?" Amy clearly hadn't followed her thought process.

Excitement building within her, she leaned over and kissed her roommate's cheek. "I love you, Amy, but you may be roommate-less again soon."

Amy's eyes widened. "What?"

Taylor hugged Amy, then pointed at the piece of art. "I need to tell him about that. I need him to know what I know."

Amy grinned. "You're headed to Chattanooga, aren't you? Wait for me! I'm going with you."

Eyeing the man sitting across from him, Jack took a sip of beer, then leaned back in his chair. He and Duffy had gone to a bar and grill along the riverfront within walking distance of the medical tent they were working the next couple of days.

The men and women competing were typically in tip-top shape, but in the process of pursuing their best times often dehydrated and injured themselves.

One of Jack's main jobs was to make sure someone was safe to go back out after an injury or collapse. These people had been training for months, years, and most would work through an injury, even if dangerous, if allowed to.

They finished off their drinks and headed

back toward where competition "headquarters" had been set up.

As they were walking, a woman caught his eye, making him think of Taylor. Not that she was ever far from his mind, but these days any platinum blonde had her popping into his head.

Only this one had his pulse pounding.

If he didn't know better, he'd swear the woman was Taylor.

Then he noticed the familiar woman with her.

Taylor was in Chattanooga and Amy was with her.

"Hey, isn't that…?" Duffy asked, sounding surprised, but not quite as authentically as he should have. Duffy must have known they were in town.

"Looks like it." He braced himself for however Taylor responded to seeing him. Had she known there was a possibility she'd bump into him here? Greg knew he was here and would have mentioned the competition to Amy. Maybe they'd all decided to drive down to check out the event. Or was Amy playing matchmaker again? Had she messaged Duffy to find them and was throwing him and Taylor together?

Taylor spotted him, looked uncertain for the briefest of seconds, then flashed a big smile on her pretty face.

A big, genuine smile. A smile that lit up his world and had every nerve cell straining to get near her. She stopped walking, her mouth dropping open.

"You cut your hair!" she pointed out unnecessarily.

He reached up, ran his palm over his bare neck. "Why are you here?"

Probably not the best intro to seeing her after two months had passed, but it's what popped out of his mouth.

"Good to see you, too," she replied, turning to Duffy and giving him a smile of his own. "Duffy, how are you?"

Duffy hugged Taylor, then Amy. Taylor gave Amy a look and, taking her cue, Amy locked her arm with Duffy's. "Let's go for a walk, my friend. We need to catch up since I missed out on seeing you at Rockin' Tyme."

Duffy didn't hesitate, just abandoned Jack with Taylor. Yeah, his friend had known Amy and Taylor were there.

"You didn't answer my question," Taylor reminded Jack once they were alone.

No, he hadn't. He glanced around them, wanting to be somewhere other than where they were. They could walk to the bridge, go to the park, but with the competition there would likely still be too many people around.

"Let's walk down to the riverbank," he suggested. There might possibly still be people around, but it would be less crowded at least.

Glancing toward the Tennessee River, Taylor nodded. "Okay, if that's what you want."

Taylor had rehearsed what she'd say to Jack a thousand times in her head on the drive to Chattanooga. Now that she was with him, had set eyes on him, she could barely string two words together.

Maybe his haircut and being clean-shaven had thrown her. She'd never seen him without his hair being long. He looked amazing, but she missed his tousled, *I don't care* look.

He wore his khaki shorts and a T-shirt—one of his Rockin' Tyme shirts, which made her smile. The shirt seemed fitting for her arrival and what she wanted to tell him. She'd acknowledged that she'd torn free of her chrysalis and emerged a different woman after her divorce. But she hadn't found her wings until Rockin' Tyme.

Until Jack.

He'd encouraged her to spread those wings and take flight, teaching her to trust in herself and soar. His voice hadn't overridden hers but had instead encouraged her, lifted her. No matter what happened, no matter what he said, she would be fine, would continue to fly.

She'd just fly higher with him beside her.

"You here for the tough-guy competition tomorrow?"

She laughed at the absolute absurdity of her competing in the event. "I'm not near tough enough for that. You?"

He grinned. "Working medical."

"What's next for you, Jack?"

He hesitated to answer and she wondered if he'd tell her to mind her own business, that he didn't want her to know his schedule or showing up where he was.

"I've a little time off coming up, then I'm headed to Las Vegas for a few weeks."

"I've never been to Las Vegas." Yeah, that had been wistfulness in her voice.

His brow arched.

"I've not been to a lot of places," she continued. "But I plan to change that."

He stared at her and she didn't blame him. She wasn't making a lot of sense.

"I'm quitting my job, Jack." Which probably didn't make sense to him either. He didn't know that she'd saved every spare dime over the past year, had quite a nice little nest egg, and if she lived tight, could get by for quite some time.

Concern twisted his face. "What? What happened?"

"You happened."

His brows drew together as he visibly tried to make sense of what she was saying.

"Warrenville will always be special," she continued. "But I want to see the world, to travel and not define myself by where I live or work."

Had she not been watching him so closely she might have missed the flash of disappointment that appeared on his face before he said, "I'm happy for you, Taylor."

That flash of disappointment nearly did her in. She didn't understand why he'd be disappointed, but she pressed onward. This was too important to lose her voice, her nerve now.

"What I want is for you to be happy for *us*, Jack."

"Us?"

Here went everything.

"You told me if I ever needed you, that I knew where to find you. Well, I've found you, Jack, so it's time for you to tell me exactly what you meant by your comment."

They'd stopped walking along the riverfront and had gone halfway down the bank between the walkway and the water.

In the moonlight and glow from the riverfront

buildings Jack studied Taylor's face, how her eyes sparkled, how her chin lifted in defiance of anyone who stood in her way.

She was beautiful.

And not saying things he was prepared to hear.

"If you need me, I'll be there. You know that."

"That's what I thought you meant. What I hoped you meant," she corrected, then met his gaze head on. "I need you, Jack."

When words failed him, she continued. "I want to travel with you, Jack. To see the world with you."

Was that what she'd meant?

Jack took a deep breath. "That may be a problem."

Taylor's face fell. "I... What kind of problem?"

A wry grin tugged at his lips. "I've recently made changes to my schedule and won't be traveling nearly as much in the future."

Uncertainty darkened her face. "What?"

"You once asked me if I ever thought of some place as home." He smiled at the memory, at his recent realization. "I never had, but now, when Warrenville comes into my head, I get nostalgic." He shrugged one shoulder. "You might say homesick."

Her mouth opened. "Oh."

Studying her, he said words he'd once not ever expected to say. "I'm coming home, Taylor."

Eyes big, full of emotion, she asked, "When?"

"As soon as this competition is over."

"You'll be in Warrenville until you leave for Las Vegas?"

"Yes." Telling her he was coming back to her felt good, felt liberating. "And I'll be back as soon as Las Vegas is over."

She swallowed. "You're moving back to Warrenville? But…"

"Is my moving back a problem for you?"

"No, but…"

He might feel good, but Taylor looked torn as she said, "But, Jack, you'll be miserable."

Taken aback at her comment, he asked, "Why on earth would I be miserable if I moved to Warrenville?"

Then it hit him, threatened to knock the wind from his chest and buckle his knees. "You're not going to be there, are you?" He could smack himself in the head. "All this to be with you and you're going to be gone."

Her lips parted, her expression brightened. "You're moving to Warrenville to be with me?"

He nodded. "It's not the town that made me homesick, Taylor. It's not being with you." He looked her straight in the eyes and told her what was in his heart. "You are what makes Warren-ville home. You are home."

Taylor could stand it no longer and closed the short distance between her and Jack, practically throwing herself into his arms.

"I've missed you so much."

She wasn't sure if she said the words or if he did, just that he lifted her off her feet and hugged her to him.

"I don't want you to get heavy feet, Jack," she told him, placing her palms on his cheeks and staring up into his eyes. "And, I sure don't want to be what weighs you down. Not ever. That's why I'm leaving Warrenville. I want to be with you, wherever you are."

"Then I guess you're going to be spending a lot of time in Warrenville."

"We don't have to stay there. I'll go with you. Really."

"That's not going to work. I've a farm to take care of."

"What?" Then it clicked, and her jaw dropped. "It was you who bought the farm, wasn't it?"

He lifted one shoulder. "I live a simple life. The farm was a good investment. Besides, I have a lot of good memories at that place."

"But…why would you buy it?" She couldn't even begin to imagine what the farm had cost him.

"Because I have to have somewhere for us to live."

"You want me to live there?"

Snorting, he ran his fingers through what was left of his hair. "I thought I had a few more days to plan this, to come up with something grand to convince you to say yes."

Taylor's heart missed a beat.

He took her hands into his. "I want you to live at the farm with me, Taylor. Or wherever it is you want to live. Wherever you are, that's where I want to be."

"Jack," she whispered, fighting back moisture that was prickling her eyes.

"Say yes, Taylor. Tell me you'll live at the farm with me."

His words about his grandparents blasted through her head and the thought of the farm becoming a gilded cage that locked away his free spirit tore at her.

"No, Jack. I won't."

Jack's ears roared. He'd thought…no matter what he'd thought. Obviously, he'd misunderstood.

He let go of her hands but she grabbed hold of his.

"I came here to find you, Jack, to tell you that wherever you are is where I want to be." Her eyes searched his. "We don't have to live at the farm or even have four walls of our own. So long as I'm with you, that's what matters."

He'd botched this. Then again, he really had thought he had longer to figure out what to say to her, to figure out what he was going to do next.

"I love you, Taylor."

Like that. He hadn't planned to just spit those words out. Had he had time to plan, he'd have come up with some elaborate way to have told her, some special way that a woman like Taylor deserved.

Her eyes widened, then softened as a smile lit up her face. "That's why I'm here, Jack." She placed both palms on his cheeks, cupping his face. "Because I love you, too."

"You do?" His ears had to have heard wrong. He'd known she cared, known they were good together, but he hadn't let himself dream that she might love him.

"Don't act as if you aren't fully aware of how I feel about you, Jack Morgan, because you know I love you."

Had he? He'd not outright thought it, but maybe she was right. Part of why he'd bought that farm was because Taylor loved him and only a fool would let that love go to waste.

Especially when that love was reciprocated a hundred-fold.

"I'm not just the rebound sex guy?" he teased, running his fingers into her hair to caress her.

"Oh, you're the rebound sex guy," she assured him. "But you're also my forever sex guy." She studied him. "My forever everything guy. If you want to be."

Jack brought her hand to his lips and pressed a kiss there. "For the record, I've never wanted anything more."

"There you go making me wonder if you're for real again," she accused as she stood on tip-toe and kissed him.

Kissed him for now and forever after.

EPILOGUE

TAYLOR WASN'T SURPRISED to see the group of guitar-picking men in front of her tent at the Rockin' Tyme music festival.

At the end of their shift in the medical tent, she and Amy had gone to wait in the shower line then wash away the day's grime.

Duffy nodded in acknowledgement of their return but kept singing about mommas and cowboys.

Taylor leaned over to kiss the top of Jack's head, brushing back a stray shoulder-length hair that had escaped his man-bun as she did so, then sat in the chair next to him to watch them play. With the songs she recognized, she sang along. Loud and carefree and full of enjoying herself. When Jack finished singing a number, she let loose with applause.

Duffy shook his head and gave a pretend disgruntled sigh. "Same groupie two years in a row."

"Same groupie rest of my life," Jack corrected,

causing the rest of the gang to launch into good-natured ribbing.

Taylor smiled. The past year had been amazing. She and Jack had moved into the farmhouse. They'd both taken PRN positions at the hospital. She went with Jack on most of his events, working at the ones she could get hired on with, and just attending the ones that hadn't needed another nurse. Her favorite so far had been car racing. She'd loved that boisterous crowd.

They'd found a happy balance of white picket fence and adventure.

Jack nurtured her need to dig, to carve away years of toxic layers to uncover who she was inside. Nurtured and, much as she did with her clay, helped her discover who she was and to embrace that woman.

Who she was loved him with all her heart.

Lost in thought, she'd missed that Jack had set his guitar aside until his getting down on one knee caught her eye.

"Jack?" Heart racing, she asked, "What are you doing?"

"What's long past due," he said, taking her hand in his and giving it a reassuring squeeze.

Her blood pounded through her veins.

"Will you marry me, Taylor?"

"Jack?" She could barely breathe and his name came out as little more than a hoarse whisper.

"Because you are the greatest adventure of my life," he continued, his eyes warm, reassuring, happy. "And I can't imagine my world without you at my side."

That he'd so perfectly echoed what she'd just been thinking, what was in her heart, Taylor couldn't hold back the moisture stinging her eyes.

"Yes!" She nodded. "Oh, yes."

"'Bout time," Duffy piped up from behind Jack.

Amy nodded her agreement. Everyone around them clapped and gave their approval as Jack stood, pulled Taylor to her feet.

"I love you," he said, kissing her.

"I'm glad," she whispered back when their lips parted. "So very glad, because you're my greatest adventure, too."

* * * * *

If you enjoyed this story, check out these other great reads from Janice Lynn

Friend, Fling, Forever?
Heart Surgeon to Single Dad
A Surgeon to Heal Her Heart
A Firefighter in Her Stocking

All available now!